My Name Is Jane Gray

My Name Is Jane Gray

By

Roger Sanderson

Other Books By Roger Sanderson

Liverpool to Las Vegas

Desert Breeze Publishing, Inc.
27305 W. Live Oak Rd #424
Castaic, CA 91384

http://www.DesertBreezePublishing.com

Copyright © 2015 by Roger Sanderson
ISBN 10: 1-61252-533-4
ISBN 13: 978-1-61252-533-4

Published in the United States of America
Publish Date: August 2015

Editor-In-Chief: Gail R. Delaney
Editor: Christy Dyer
Marketing Director: Jenifer Ranieri
Cover Artist: Gwen Phifer

Cover Art Copyright by Desert Breeze Publishing, Inc © 2015

All rights reserved. No portion of this book may be reproduced or transmitted in any form or by any electronic or mechanical means, including photocopying, recording or by any information retrieval and storage system without permission of the publisher.

Names, characters and incidents depicted in this book are products of the author's imagination, or are used in a fictitious situation. Any resemblances to actual events, locations, organizations, incidents or persons – living or dead – are coincidental and beyond the intent of the author.

Dedication and Acknowledgment

For Jake James, with love

Beginning

This must be the good life, thought Jane Gray. Since she was only in San Francisco for a year, there was no point trying to put down roots. The firm had leased her a flat and a car. She chose a flat in Sausalito and asked for a Jaguar like the one she'd sold in England, but a red one this time.

However, she didn't drive to work. Sausalito was just across the Bay from the business centre of the city so she took the ferry every morning. Commuting to work by boat, seeing the shining buildings of San Francisco grow steadily larger as she approached them was magic. Every day the weather was different.

She had acquaintances on the boat, mostly business people. She didn't stand out, there were other women like her; smart, well-dressed, obviously in high-powered jobs. They exchanged brisk smiles and sat with a coffee to hand and a laptop on their laps. Executive women were accepted here in America just as they were beginning to be in England.

It was four months since she'd arrived. She enjoyed the work as a director of Walter G. Traekel (Training) Inc. It was a very responsible position. Walter believed in letting his staff make decisions. She had made a number of changes in the organisation and thought they were working well. She'd also run a few courses herself. That had been one of her stipulations -- it was important to her.

Her social life was good too. She was a member of the team, they did things together. She had taken weekend trips to Yosemite, flown to Las Vegas, walked along the rock-bound Northern coast. Her flat in Sausalito had a balcony overlooking the Bay that was big enough to hold a table and chairs. She had held dinner parties there.

She had even dated a couple of men. Mind you, she thought the word "dated" was appalling, she was forty-one, not sixteen. However, it was the term everyone used, so she went along with it. A night at the ballet, or the opera, dinner afterward at Fisherman's Wharf. Both men were friends of friends -- charming, educated, and good company. Both wanted a relationship to develop, but nothing would come of either of them. She didn't want it to.

It was only a six minute walk from the ferry terminal to her particular glass-sided skyscraper and then a swift journey to the twenty-seventh floor. She sat at her desk, glanced at the wonderful view -- sea, ships, hills, bridges. It was always comfortable in her seat. The air conditioning never faltered, the glass darkened automatically if the sun got too strong.

She seemed to have everything. This was what she'd worked for. So why was she not happy?

She turned to her terminal, tapped in her password, and remembered...

Chapter One

"My name is Jane Gray," replied Jane, raising her voice slightly over the noise of the party. She looked at Alan and guessed he was in his late twenties. He was obviously relieved she was prepared to be friendly. As he'd approached there had been a touch of bravado in his manner, a slight embarrassment as he introduced himself to her. After all, she was an "older woman" and a very well dressed one too.

"Can I fetch you a drink, Jane?" he asked. "What would you like?"

He took her glass as she said, "I'd really prefer dry white wine, but if there's only that awful punch left, I'll risk it."

"I'm sure there'll be some wine. Be right back." A shy, rather abashed smile and he made for the makeshift bar at the back of the Everett Products staff canteen. He was tall, lithe, well-balanced, better at moving through a crowd than he was at standing still talking to older, frightening women. She wondered if he was a sportsman -- rugby perhaps, or squash.

Anyway, she would soon be able to leave. As work parties go, it hadn't been bad, but she much preferred doing business in an office or over lunch. So far she had nodded to the managing director, accepted a drink from the training manager, and had a couple of stilted conversations with people she'd taught. She might be wearing a little black dress instead of her customary suit but she was still here as a consultant, not a woman and so far this had not been her idea of a good time.

Alan returned, a drink in each hand, swerving expertly round a boisterous group for whom the free food and drink was obviously something to be cherished. Handing her a glass, he said, "I looked under the drinks table. There appeared to be bottles people had forgotten about."

Jane smiled. Obviously this man had been to office parties before. She sipped her drink and waited. He had come over to her, she wanted to see how he handled the next move. If he said something crass, like, "are you on your own?" then she'd go at once.

In fact he was reasonably subtle. "I've only worked here for eighteen months and as I'm buried in the computer room I don't get to meet many people. Which section do you work for?"

"I don't work for a section, I'm a consultant. My firm is running a series of training courses for middle and top management and the MD invited me to this party." Even in party gear Jane always carried business cards, so she fished one out of her handbag and offered it to him. Pure white, engraved in black. *Jane Gray Associates,* with office address, e-mail, telephone, and fax numbers. It looked impressive. She had intended it to.

"So it's your own firm. I've seen the notices about the courses. They look useful. Do you do any training yourself or are you purely an administrator?"

It was a good question. He'd shown he was interested. There might be something worth salvaging in an evening that had so far been a very poor use of her time. She would like a few minutes of intelligent conversation.

Before answering, though, she paused and looked at him a little more closely. He knew what she was doing and accepted it with a half-smile. She'd already decided that if he blushed or looked uneasy he could go back and join the other boys. If he preened, thinking he'd made a conquest, then likewise. But so far he was doing well.

"I still do some training," she said, "but not as often as I'd like to. It's important never to lose the edge, never to forget what being in the front of a group is like."

She was tall and wearing heels but he overtopped her. As she'd noticed, he had the ease and presence of an athlete, of a man who is at home with his own body. Perhaps his neck was a little too thick and his face certainly wasn't handsome -- his mother might have called it rough-hewn -- but his smile was gentle and his bright green eyes sparkled.

Most of all Jane liked his voice. Voices were important to her, both professionally and personally. Alan's voice was deep and clear and as he spoke there were undertones of humour.

Then he said, "Do you run courses on body language, Jane?"

What had made him ask that? "I don't give them in person," she said cautiously, "and I feel that a session on body language is only useful as a part of something larger. But yes, I do offer such things."

"So what is your body saying now?"

That was a challenge! Jane stood slightly more upright and stared at him. Occasionally on a course you got awkward or self-opinionated members who had to be muted for the good of the rest. She rarely had a problem with that. Alan smiled back at her, unperturbed.

Her first reaction was to snap at him that her body was intimating she was bored with his company, but it struck her that she wasn't bored and this young man's question had been perceptive. She had indeed been looking at him in a way that was dispassionate, if not exactly critical. Unusually -- very unusual for her -- she felt a tiny bit guilty and as a result she giggled. "Sorry. Was I staring at you?"

"You were. You were looking at me in a manner I can only call assessing. Howard over there looks at me that way when I ask for more money for back-up drives."

Howard Metcalfe was the managing director, but Alan didn't use his name with any degree of bravado. They were obviously on Christian name terms.

"I'll let you loose on my computer to make up for it," she said lightly, "and I apologise for staring. Sorry, Alan, I didn't catch your surname."

"Alan Murray. I'm in charge of the computing department. Systems analysis, project management, that kind of thing."

"Very impressive," she said truthfully. "My firm has never had anything to do with your section. What are you working on at present?"

He shrugged. "Oh, I mess about with production figures and flow charts and so on. A smidgeon of development. A bit of work for other branches."

Jane raised her eyebrows. "That's a nice vague answer that doesn't say very much. Either you've got a nothing job -- the computer equivalent of making the tea -- or you're very important."

There was a touch of awkwardness in his expression when he answered, but Jane thought it was because his attempt at playing down the truth had been detected. He was quietly confident when he said, "I suppose 'very important' is nearest."

"I do run courses on security," she replied. "I'll not ask you for any further details."

A man managing to hold two glasses in each hand muttered "excuse me" and tried to sidle behind Alan. Alan put his hand gently on her shoulder and moved toward her to let him pass. For a moment their bodies were close, even touching, and she found the tiny intimacy surprisingly exciting.

She had a better sense of smell than most people. She could tell he was wearing expensive cologne -- Armani perhaps -- but underneath she detected the warmth of his body. His clothes were delightfully fresh. Many of the suits she'd been close to tonight had smelt wardrobe-musty. One had even smelt of mothballs.

He murmured "Arpege" and she was astounded. Only one man in ten thousand could recognise scent, especially her rather unusual one. So when they were close and she was reacting to his warmth, he was doing exactly the same with her. She tried to put the realisation from her mind.

"You're quite right," she said. "Well done."

They moved apart. His suit was good, a dark blue worsted of conventional cut, obviously tailor fitted. The white shirt was heavy silk. Only the tie showed the ebullience of youth, a chaotic pattern of crimson, emerald, and black. He had presence.

They were standing by the wall. He waved his hand to the centre of the room. "Would you like to dance, Jane?" In a tiny cleared space, far too many couples were holding each other, jigging up and down and wearing paper hats. The DJ shouted encouragement.

"Yes, I would like to dance. But it doesn't look possible here."

"Then let me ask you a more exact question. Would you like to stand on the dance-floor and wriggle in close proximity to my body and approximately in time to the music?"

He had an ear for words, she appreciated witty men. But still she said, "The offer is appealing but I feel I must resist. Perhaps the next waltz?"

"I don't think I can wait," he said and they both laughed.

The staff of Everett Products had done their best to decorate the works canteen for their summer extravaganza. There were soft lights, streamers, balloons, and a light show. They couldn't fix the proportions of the room though, so it still came across as rather spartan. *They would have done better*, Jane thought, *to have made the dance floor bigger.*

As is usual in office parties most people stuck firmly to their own group. "Are those your colleagues?" Jane asked Alan, nodding at the table she thought he had come from.

"Yes, that's the computer department. Would you like to join them? They'd be delighted."

"I'd hate to cramp their style," she said, watching one of them arrive back at the table with a tray full of drinks. Everyone seemed to need at least two. She went on, "I wouldn't want to interfere with their dedication to the task in hand."

"Shame on you. That's both catty and accurate."

As if to prove her point, one of Alan's team lifted a pint glass, pointed to it, and waved questioningly in their direction. Alan shook his head and smiled. The whole group were young, male, and speedily getting drunk. They all looked like geeks. One was even wearing a spotted bow tie. "Do you not have any women in your department?" she asked.

"I certainly do. They'll be around somewhere. Those are the lads whose partners were too sensible to come tonight. You're unusual, Jane," he added. "You're the only person here who isn't with a group. Don't you feel a bit out of things?"

She shook her head. "I could have brought a partner but I didn't feel the need. I was invited to sit with the training manager and his family, but I said I'd rather circulate and meet a few of the people I'd trained."

"I see." He grinned, a boyish expression that suddenly reminded her that she was older than him. "I saw you from over there. You looked alone but not lonely, perfectly self-possessed and you were the most attractive woman in the room."

"Flattery," she said, "will get you anywhere." It was meant as a light-hearted answer, but she found herself hoping he meant what he said. Whether she meant what she said was another question.

They gazed round the room again. The party seemed to be a success, everyone was enjoying themselves. One or two people were working the room, deliberately calling at every table to say something friendly.

"Here comes our managing director," said Alan. "It looks as if it's your turn for the allocated four minutes of good cheer." It was an observation, not a criticism.

Sure enough, Howard was making his way toward them. "It might be you he wants to talk to," suggested Jane.

"I doubt it. He dealt with our table first. Got in early while people were still sober."

Jane grinned. "He's a shrewd man."

Howard Metcalfe had given her one of her earliest big contracts. Over the past five years he had doubled the turnover of Everett Products and the growth seemed sustainable. When he wanted to please her, he said that much of the growth was due to her firm's training. To a certain extent she thought he was right.

"Lovely party, Howard," she said. "I hear you've got cause to celebrate. Congratulations on the new lines." A new set of freeze-dried foods was currently sweeping the markets.

"Thank you. Partly due to you, you know. It's good to see you here."

"I'll settle for a share of the profits." They both laughed.

Alan had withdrawn a little. He obviously couldn't work out the relationship between Howard and her. Being a good manager, Howard promptly hauled him back into the conversation. "You've been introduced to Miss Gray then, Alan?"

"I introduced myself. She's a guest at our works party and her glass was empty."

"Was it now? Just like mine? Did I see you find a bottle under the table?" With a smile, Howard looked down at his glass.

Alan heaved an exaggerated sigh. "Computer expert one minute, bartender the next. May a fetch you a drink ... sir?"

"Most kind," Howard beamed.

Alan looked at her but she shook her head. She'd had her ration for the evening. He disappeared to the bar.

"He seems a bright young man," said Jane casually.

"He's one of the best, he'll go far. I picked him myself."

"Speaks well and has a good presence. Could I use him at all?"

"Find your own workers and don't poach mine, Jane."

It was said in a friendly fashion but there was still a warning there. This Alan Murray must be really good. Jane smiled and pressed on, "Not even to give the odd lecture?"

"Leave the boy alone, he's got enough to do working for me. Met anyone else interesting?"

"Depends what you mean by interesting. I was told earlier, with drunken but excruciating honesty, what was wrong with my last course."

"Who by?" The question was rapped out.

"It doesn't matter. On reflection, I think the man might have a point. I'm going to think about it."

Alan returned with two drinks and after a couple of minutes of general chat Howard said, "Come and say hello to Marion, Jane. She's always asking after you."

Marion was Howard's wife. The invitation did not seem to include Alan. So she smiled at him, thanked him for finding the decent wine, and let Howard lead her to his table.

Over the next quarter of an hour she occasionally glimpsed Alan on the other side of the room. He'd joined his friends but seemed irresolute and was not joining in their rather rowdy fun.

She enjoyed her chat with Marion, but Howard was soon off on his rounds again and when their son and his fiancée came to the table she decided it was time to go.

At the door she turned, caught Alan's eye, and waved goodbye. He was a pleasant young man. As she negotiated for her coat and umbrella at the cloakroom she was surprised when there was the rattle of feet and Alan appeared.

"Jane, if you have to go, perhaps we could share a taxi."

"I came by car," she explained, and held out her hand. "Goodnight. It was nice meeting you."

"I wondered if we might spend a little time together. I've enjoyed talking to you."

"I've enjoyed talking to you too. However, I'm flying down to London tomorrow morning and I have to sort out some papers first."

She could tell he was one of Howard's lads. The moment she mentioned paperwork, he understood. Work comes before everything.

"I hope we'll meet again soon."

"I'm sure we'll bump into each other around the place. Don't get wet now. Bye." She opened her umbrella and dashed out into the rainy car park.

When she reached her car she looked back and Alan Murray was still in the illuminated foyer, peering out. She almost had a lunatic desire to turn round and spend more time with him. She didn't. It wasn't her, not the Jane Gray she had worked so hard to create.

Instead she climbed into her car and switched on the ignition. It was late summer, but still a dark, rainy, windy night. Suitable for ships to pass in.

*****

Jane drove quite a lot during the course of her work. She enjoyed it and she could get tax relief on the car. So every three years she leased a new Jaguar. Just the smallest, the XF CE. It was a sensual pleasure to sit inside, to smell that subtle aroma that only expensive cars seem to have. Her present one was dark grey, a little joke on her part.

She listened to the murmur of the engine and then slipped a disc into the music centre. For some reason she was feeling discontented.

The richness of Mozart's "Wind Octet" filled the car but even that didn't still her restlessness.

Instead of turning right onto the main road she turned left and followed a winding cul-de-sac. She'd been here before. It was a good place to think. At the end was a small parking area, a low wall, and over that was an uninterrupted view of the river. She was alone for once, there were no love-making couples in anonymous cars keeping her company tonight.

Jane parked and watched the dark moving river, the lights on the far bank, the silhouette of a ship edged with lights, moving slowly upstream. Rain was beating and rattling on her windscreen; usually this calmed her, but now it added to her feeling of something unfinished.

As she drove back past the canteen she saw a dark figure stride out of the car park. There was something about the easy gait that she recognised. She drove on fifty yards then stopped and reversed. Opening her window, she shouted, "Do you think women should pick up strangers at night?"

"You'll find me no trouble," said Alan Murray and loped round to get in the passenger door. As he climbed in Jane tried to tell herself she'd stopped out of perverseness; because Howard Metcalfe had warned her off. She wasn't usually bad though, it was counter-productive. She realised Alan had had more of an effect on her than she'd thought.

"You didn't fancy staying for the rest of the festivities?" she asked.

In the darkness he shook his head and drops of rain flicked from his hair onto her face. She rather liked it. He said, "I didn't want to get drunk and after you left there was no one I wanted to talk to."

She wondered if he thought she'd been waiting outside for him. She was not going to explain her actions. She was still unsure of them herself.

He told her he lived in one of the villages now swallowed up by the ever-expanding city. The suburban line running south down the river passed through it. He had intended to get a taxi to the nearest station.

She had a swift internal debate with herself and said, "I live close to a station on that line. Would you like to come for a coffee for an hour? Then you can walk to catch your train."

"I'd really like that," he said.

She wondered why she'd made the offer. She thought he might be wondering the same thing.

*****

The wet streets were largely deserted and it didn't take her long to drive through the industrial estate and onto the arterial road paralleling the river.

Paradine House was a single block of flats built on the site of an old merchant's house. It looked out across the sand dunes to the main channel of the river. There were only twelve flats. She had one of the two penthouses.

"You live here?" he asked incredulously as she worked the electronic system and drove into the underground garage.

"You didn't think I lived in a bed-sitter somewhere did you?" she asked. "There's no mystery to it. When I was twenty-two I put down every available penny on a house I couldn't afford. My house doubled in price over the next five years so I did the same again. It's not hard to stay ahead in housing once you have a start."

"Your house doubled in price over five years?"

"One of the dubious benefits of being my age is that I've lived through some strange economic times."

He laughed. "Jane, you're being ageist. Are you going to tell me how old you are?"

"Forty-one next birthday. You?"

"I'm twenty-eight," he said it without expression but she suspected she'd made him think. That was possibly a good thing.

He was silent as they rode up in the lift to her penthouse on the fourth floor. She unlocked the front door and then, without putting on a light, opened the twin doors of the little vestibule. There was a quick intake of breath but he remained silent.

Her living room was twice the normal height and the far wall was one great double-glazed window. The room appeared to float above the sand dunes, the shore, the great river and the far-distant hills. Now all that could be seen were dim lights and the reflected sheen on the dark water. It seemed even more remote.

She clicked on the wall lights. He stood in the middle of the room slowly looking round as if he couldn't believe it. It pleased her that he didn't try to hide his amazement under a show of glib sophistication.

"This is a really fine room, Jane. It's beautiful."

"I'm a successful, unmarried, middle-aged woman. This is what I choose to spend my money on."

He looked round. Because of the ever-changing views she had kept things minimalist, there was charcoal carpeting, blonde wood-panelling on the walls and little furniture. He said, "I think you could have made even that bed-sitter look well."

It was a graceful compliment. "Not all of it was my idea," she explained, "I was helped by..."

A door to one side of the room opened and a voice said, "Jane, I'm so sorry. I didn't know you had a visitor."

They turned. A man looked at them with a self-deprecating smile. He was aged about fifty, with an erect trim figure and unusually long silver hair. He wore a white shirt and his feet were bare.

"I was about to say," continued Jane, "that most of the good ideas in this room came from someone else. It was this man, Claude Driscoll. Claude, meet Alan Murray."

It had always been one of her strengths as a trainer that she could take a detached view of a situation in which people thought she should be involved. She found it amusing. Poor Alan didn't know what to think. Was he a cuckoo in a love-nest? Claude's bare feet, her lack of surprise, the fact that this man had helped to design the flat. Did she live with him?

Meanwhile, Claude and Alan were doing the things men do; shaking hands, mumbling platitudes, assessing each other covertly.

"I've brought Alan back for a coffee," she explained. "He's waiting for a train."

"An excellent idea. I made a pot some minutes ago. We can all have some. Alan, let me take your coat."

Claude whisked away the bemused Alan's coat and winked at Jane wickedly from behind his back. She sat in silence with Alan until Claude bustled back with the coffee. He poured for all three of them, then took his cup and said, "I've ten minutes more work and then I must go. Nice to meet you, Alan, hopefully we'll have longer to chat next time." The door to Jane's study closed softly behind him.

"Seems a nice chap," offered Alan tentatively.

Jane didn't think she'd ever heard a request for reassurance put so gingerly. She decided she'd been unfair. "He was teasing you. Claude is my second in command. He often works here when the office is closed. He has a key."

"I see," said Alan, indicating that he did not.

"Claude is a very, very good friend of mine -- and he is gay. His partner is an architect. Apparently they can be extremely temperamental, which is why Claude prefers to be anywhere but at home when Gavin has a deadline."

Alan's next action disconcerted her. He slid to her end of the couch, grasped her by the shoulders, and kissed her. She didn't know what to think. She hadn't been kissed like that in years, and she was shocked at the strength of her response.

He released her and said ruefully, "That was an act of rampant male aggression. But you were getting at me, weren't you?"

She caught her breath and then she had to laugh. "I suppose so."

"I did enjoy kissing you."

Time to move to a different tone. Lightly, she said, "Kissing me is like kissing a nun. It's all right as long as you don't get into the habit."

He winced. "Jane, I remember when I first heard that joke. I thought it was incredibly worldly. I was nine at the time."

Suddenly, she felt remarkably old.

By unspoken consent they enjoyed a few minutes of companionable silence, sipping coffee and watching the riding lights of a ship inching down the channel. Claude came back into the room, now dressed in camel-hair overcoat and fortunately wearing shoes. "Finished. I've left the report on the desk, Jane."

"Thank you. I hope Gavin is in a better temper by the time you get back."

"Couldn't be worse," said Claude. "I'll ring you early tomorrow before you go. I'll let myself out. Hope to see you again, Alan." He was gone.

There was a change in the atmosphere that was almost palpable. *Pheromones,* thought Jane to herself, *they cause all the trouble in the world.* "Tell me where you trained, Alan," she said.

He smiled. "Lesson one. If a lady feels that a young man is about to become importunate, she should ask him to talk about himself. Few men can resist this invitation and the conversation may be steered into more ... fruitful channels."

Solemnly she clapped. "Such an old head on such young shoulders. Where did you learn that?"

At Cambridge, as she might have guessed. He'd got a double first and won assorted prizes for mathematics. She got the impression that most of the time he had worked on his own projects. He had that focused narrow-mindedness of the obsessed intellectual. Yet his body was in very good shape, he obviously exercised regularly. She was a trained good listener but she was fascinated by what he told her of a computeled future. She would have to ask Howard Metcalfe again if she could use him for an occasional lecture.

"So that's the Alan Murray saga," he finished. "You now know my strengths, my weaknesses, my dreams, hopes, plans. I'd like to know you equally well, please."

"You've told me things," she pointed out. "That doesn't mean that I know you."

"I'm hoping you will in time. Tell me about yourself. Were you ever married?"

She shook her head. "Would you have asked a man that question? No, like you I've always been married to my work. I've had relationships of course. I've had offers, I've had lovers, but never a man I desperately needed to live with. I like men, but when I see my female friends falling in love, it always seems so messy. I'm still having a good life."

Once again the conversation seemed to be taking a wrong turn so she told him about her early life as a training officer, and how she had developed Jane Gray Associates until it was the largest training organisation in the north of England. It was the traditional, successful businesswoman's story. All good boring stuff, but he appeared to be fascinated. Warning bells were ringing in Jane's head.

She made a point of looking at her watch and asked, "What time is your train? You don't want to miss it."

He glanced reluctantly at his own watch and for a moment she thought he might contradict her. He sighed. "It's in twenty minutes. If I'm to catch it I ought to leave now." But he made no move.

"You are going to catch it," said Jane. "Since it's raining, I'll run you to the station."

They were side by side on the couch. He turned and moved toward her.

"Don't," she said.

There was a moment's fraught pause. Then he said, "Jane, it's been very pleasant having coffee with you. You've turned a standard party into an enjoyable evening. Do you think Claude hung my coat in your kitchen?" He stood and looked at her enquiringly.

She was impressed. He had taken her rejection like a gentleman, converted what could have been unpleasant into nothing. She fetched his coat.

They drew up outside the station and he opened his door at once. "Thanks once again, Jane, it's been lovely meeting you. May I see you again some time?"

"I'll be at Everetts for a couple of days next week. We might bump into each other," she said pleasantly. She didn't want him making assumptions.

"Goodnight then." He shut the door carefully and she drove away.

Back at home she looked at the figures Claude had been checking and worked through them herself. It was three o'clock in the morning before fatigue drove her to bed. Silly of her when she had to get up early. She'd known the calculations would be fine. They didn't need to be re-done.

She realised she had been working to stop thinking of Alan Murray.

Chapter Two

Jane never had difficulty waking, no matter how little sleep she'd had. The discreet alarm rang and she swung her feet out of bed before it stopped. It was part of her routine, routine kept her happy. She liked to follow a predetermined course and think about what she had to do in the day. This morning however, she was irritated. Unnecessary memories of Alan Murray interfered with more important considerations and she couldn't get him out of her head.

Routine, she told herself. First the power shower, five minutes in front of the mirror for her hair, then she weighed herself. Good, no change. Whenever she was more than four pounds over what was acceptable to her, she went on a month's gentle diet.

She pulled the duvet together and made the bed. There was nothing more slovenly than an unmade bed.

Then it was honesty time. Two folding doors pulled out from her built-in wardrobe to form an alcove. She took off her dressing gown and stood naked in the alcove. Now she was surrounded with mirrors and illuminated by lights shining from the tops of the doors.

Her body wasn't bad. She tried to check all of it, squeezing where there might be spare flesh. Her waist was trim, her breasts still firm, but she couldn't go without a bra as she had when she was twenty. She guessed she would do.

She stood still, pressed a switch, and lights flashed four times. She had photographed herself. She started when she was twenty-three. She had taken photographs every two years and now she had nine sets stored away. It was a progression that marked the development -- if not the deterioration -- of her body.

Jane dressed rapidly. Like all her clothes, her underwear was expensive. It made her feel good. It made her feel successful. For the visible layer, she chose a shirt with a white jabot and a dark suit. She looked neat, orderly, and professional.

Into the study to pick up her already packed briefcase. It too was tidy. It was now seven o'clock. Her taxi drew up as she walked out of the front door. The firm she used knew she insisted on it arriving dead on time.

She arrived at the airport with plenty of time to spare and bought the Financial Times. It was only an hour's flight to London. There was no need to go over the papers in her briefcase. She knew the contents already.

She was met by a blue-suited chauffeur who drove her through the city to the underground garage of Ledsham's Merchant Bank. Here she was greeted in soft tones by Francis Dartington, a partner of the old school, in a starched collar and a six button double breasted suit to prove it. He called her "my dear Miss Gray," trusted she had had a comfortable journey, and escorted her to the conference chamber. This was all old, dark, polished wood and heavy upholstery. Jane hid a smile at the sight of modern computer screens looking out of place in this Edwardian elegance.

Francis offered her sherry and a slice of fruitcake. He looked slightly pained when there was an explosion of excitement at the other end of the room. Someone was making altogether too much of opening a door and walking through it.

A man entered. The suit was nearly white and the tie apparently represented an atomic explosion. The sixty-year-old face above it was completely alert. Francis murmured, "May I introduce you to the third party of our little plot. This is Walter G. Traekel."

"Miss Gray," boomed Walter G. "I've read everything you've sent me with great interest. It sure is a pleasure to meet you."

Jane shook the offered hand and said, "I've read about you too, Mr Traekel -- both the papers you've sent and what I've researched."

A small predatory smile indicated Walter G. was no fool. With absolutely no sexual innuendo he said, "Francis here thinks he can put us in bed together. With you covering Britain and Europe and me covering the Americas, I think we can do a lot of business and earn a lot of money."

Jane smiled too. "Let's talk about it."

*****

It pained Francis to send out for mere sandwiches, but Jane and Walter refused to stop for lunch. By late afternoon they were shaking hands on a deal. Their lawyers would have a bonanza sorting out the details but they knew where they stood. Jane Gray Associates was being swallowed by an international firm. But Jane would be a director. She would be given a vast bundle of shares, share options, and perks. All her staff would be kept on and all would do well out of the change. Jane herself would be given a ridiculously large lump sum, but was assured it would be structured to take maximum advantage of the tax laws.

"I'd like you to spend some time with our home operation, Jane. I think at least six months, preferably twelve. You can be based either in Boston or San Francisco."

"As soon as I can," she promised. "It's a good idea. Will you send someone to learn about our side?"

There were more arrangements to be made but Francis said he would deal with the details so he summoned the car and sent her back to the airport. Once there she phoned Claude. She hadn't wanted to do it in Francis's office. It didn't do to appear too excited.

Claude was quietly pleased and added that he'd put something for her in her flat, but wouldn't say what.

Back at home, the first thing she saw was a large bunch of red roses arranged tastefully in a vase on her coffee table. There was an envelope balanced on top. The card inside was not from Claude. It enclosed a letter and a telephone number.

> *I got tongue-tied when I phoned your number and a cool voice instructed me to leave my name, telephone number, and a brief message, so I phoned your office. Claude remembered me and offered to bring round these flowers and a letter (I like Claude).*
>
> *I enjoyed last night and hope you did too. I think we have interests in common and I would like to know you better. Could I take you to dinner? Tonight would be perfect but any time in the next week would be fine. If you phone me you'll talk to a real person, not a machine.*
>
> *With -- love? Alan.*

Hmmm. Jane read the note twice and then bent to smell the roses. They were exquisite. Then she went to her bedroom and stripped off her clothes which were travel-sticky. After a shower, she phoned Claude. "I could do without this kind of problem," she said.

Claude was amused. "I see no problem. He is attracted to you and he's a very personable young man. Persuasive too."

She pointed out, "If I need a man -- which I doubt -- I don't want a young one. I think my target range is what is called early middle age."

"Age makes very little difference, Jane. Don't be so conventional."

"Me? Conventional?"

"I thought that would irritate you. Just ask yourself if you're doing what you want or what you think other people might expect of you." He paused a moment and then went on "That's a terrible sentence but the sense is there. One more thing."

"Yes?"

"If you go to San Francisco I want to visit and wear flowers in my hair. Tell him you'll go to dinner."

It had been a full day, perhaps she was entitled to a treat. She checked her watch. It was only half past five. She stared out at her view and thought.

Alan Murray was a pleasant young man. She enjoyed his company and would like to have dinner with him. Perhaps she could recruit him too? She never stopped looking for first class tutors. That was a fair basis for having dinner, but she suspected he wanted something more than dinner. A love affair?

The very term toy-boy filled her with anger. Quite a lot of her male colleagues and acquaintances -- smart, driven men in their forties and fifties -- had younger lovers. They were regarded with covert admiration by their male friends. Why shouldn't she do what they do? The reason was that she had a horror of looking ridiculous. What is more ridiculous than a woman partnered by a man thirteen years her junior?

Her emotions were under control, just as her life was under control. She told herself that if her emotions were under control then she could easily deal with Alan Murray. Of course, she might have been reading the signs all wrong. She picked up the phone and dialled his number.

"Alan Murray here."

Voices are different on the phone but she still experienced a frisson when she heard his. It was deep and comforting. It was a voice that gave her confidence.

"Alan, it's Jane Gray. Thanks for the flowers. Aren't they a bit traditional for a young man?"

He laughed. "Any trick will do when you're trying to sweep a young girl off her feet. How was London?"

"Busy as ever." Her business in London had nothing to do with him, and she didn't want to comment on his description of her as a young girl. "I've had an invitation to visit the States."

"Not right now I trust? Jane, it's nice of you to call and I'm hoping you're phoning to say you'll have dinner with me tonight. It's six now, could I pick you up at seven?"

The minute the question came she realised she still hadn't made up her mind. This wasn't like her. She paused then said yes.

"Good. I feel there's a lot we can talk about." He sounded pleased but there was no element of triumph in his voice. "There's a pub about three-quarters of an hour's drive from your flat. The described ambiance is casual smart."

"Looking forward to it. About seven then."

Alan Murray intrigued her. He was an acknowledged computer genius and the few of them she'd met hadn't been noted for their interpersonal skills. Yet Alan had enough subtlety to indicate dress-style to her to save embarrassment later. There was more to him than she'd thought.

Talking of which, it was to be a purely social evening. She didn't have to impress anyone. No need for the dark, perfectly cut business suit, but she decided she'd still look good.

There were two sets of wardrobes in her bedroom. In one were her business clothes -- suits, mostly dark, all tailor-made. The business world appreciated good tailoring. In the other wardrobe were her sports and casual clothes. Not so many of these, she didn't seem to relax very often.

There was still enough to make a choice difficult. Finally she decided on a soft wool dress with a cowl neckline. It was in an odd grey-green shade. She had bought it in Paris a year before. With it she wore a necklace in three different shades of gold.

He was exactly on time, the buzzer rang at one minute to seven. Her monitor showed him waiting below so she pressed the door release and called through the intercom for him to come straight up. He looked at the camera above him and waved.

She went to open her front door. She was amazed to find that she was slightly nervous. Her, nervous? She was Jane Gray, forty-one-years-old, she'd been meeting and entertaining more important people than Alan Murray for the past ten years. She was still slightly nervous.

The lift light winked. This was only the second time she had ever met him. There had been occasions in the past when an impression formed in the evening wasn't fulfilled the next day. Would this be another? Would she like him as much? For that matter, would he be disappointed when he saw her? This thought she found annoying. The lift doors sighed open and they looked at each other warily.

There was the same impression of an athletic body, of a cheerfully homespun face and then of a voice like dark silk. Tonight he was wearing a fawn suit, and a dark blue shirt. She was pleased to see he wasn't wearing a medallion. She didn't like jewellery on men.

"Jane, if it's possible, you look even more gorgeous than last night," he said it with a smile so she knew he was exaggerating, but she appreciated the light tone.

"Thank you, kind sir," she said "I would curtsey demurely but I'm not wearing a flowing skirt. Come in. Would you like a glass of wine before we go?"

He sat on her couch again and she fetched two glasses of wine. It was something to do till they got over their tiny initial nervousness. They sipped the wine and didn't say very much. She wondered how the evening would progress.

After each had finished their glass, Alan offered his arm as they made their way to his car. His car was a BMW about two years old, clean and well-looked after but obviously the car of a man who needed reliable transport and nothing else. He opened the door for her and they set off north. His driving was good but not flashy, the car was a tool not a means of proving something.

He pointed to a rack of discs. "I brought some of my choice of music -- why don't you flip through."

Bach's B Minor Mass, Handel's Messiah, two or three Mozart operas. He liked the same composers as she did -- those whose music was mathematically perfect. But he was more interested in choral music. She wondered what to make of this. She liked the clarity and precision of classical instrumental music. Did he prefer something a little more human?

"Where are we going?" she asked.

"For the moment I'll keep it a secret. I want to surprise you. Yesterday I travelled to your flat at your invitation. Tonight I feel the need to assert my masculinity. I want to be in charge!"

"There might be problems taking me to an unknown distant romantic rendezvous," she pointed out. "What if last week's lover took me to the same place?"

He accepted this with aplomb. "It's a generous-minded place. I'm sure this week's lover will be served just as well." He paused a moment and then said, "Who was last week's lover?"

"Sorry, his name slips my mind. They do, you know."

He sighed "And they say romance is dead. I shall resurrect it."

If they were fencing then just for a moment his guard had dropped. She thought he meant what he had just said. It was time to stop the witty talk before it became serious. She picked out a disc. "May I put this on?"

"Of course."

They listened to the *Magic Flute*. Out of the city the road climbed through an attractive area where hills and old industries co-existed. There was plenty to look at even though it was dark and she had had a full day. Conversation lapsed.

They drove into a small hill town that had obviously had economic problems but was now on its way up. He parked in a courtyard, all designer cobbles, dark stone, and brick. A discreet sign said Harvey's Mill.

Jane had heard of Harvey's Mill but never visited it. An old works building that had been carefully, tastefully, and expensively rebuilt. As they drove in she said, "I was expecting a small pub in the hills where we could eat a bar meal. I didn't think you'd bring me somewhere like this. Are you trying to impress me?"

He came around to open her door. "Very much so."

"Why?"

He took her arm as they walked over the cobbles toward the dark glass doors set between great stone pillars. Lightly he said, "I might want your money, might want a job, I might want the pleasure of your body, or I might want the pleasure of your company. I might want some or all of these in equal or unequal amounts. You must decide which, Jane."

When she was younger, she'd known the only answer to a remark like that was to lift a quizzical eyebrow. She'd even practised. She was no good at it then and was still no good at it. "At times you do go on," she said. After all, she had to say something.

It hit her as he opened the door. She was dining with a much younger man, what would people think? All she could do was look unconcerned, but it took an effort.

They were conducted to an alcove overlooking a canal basin. There were wharfs, cranes, warehouses, brightly painted barges. Unobtrusive lights picked out what was interesting and the reflections danced on the dark waters. It was a romantic scene.

They were given menus and a wine list and asked if they wanted a drink. Jane asked for a gin and tonic, Alan ordered a pint of beer. "I have to drive," he explained. "Besides, I like beer." As he grinned he looked younger and she remembered again the thirteen years that separated them.

"All rugby players drink beer," she said.

"How did you know I played rugby? You've been asking questions about me. That's nice."

Shaking her head, she told him, "It was an informed guess. Something to do with the way you move -- and perhaps your re-arranged nose."

"She has been looking at my body," he murmured, gratified.

They ordered their meal when the waiter returned with their drinks. The menu was not too large, which was a good sign. Then they waited -- and talked.

It was twenty minutes before they were called to their table by the great glass windows and as they moved over she realised she was ravenous. She'd been through a lot that day and eaten only the odd sandwich. She was looking forward to her meal.

"Another drink?" asked Alan. "I'm going to have one more pint of beer and that will be all. But how about wine for you?"

After a small argument he ordered her a half bottle of Chablis -- not a glass. *It would do very nicely*, she thought.

They both had a salmon and prawn timbale to start with and then she had grilled mullet while he had pan fried fillet of beef. After a while they both got that feeling of contentment that comes with good food well served in good company. She was enjoying herself.

He told her more about his vision of the future of computers. She knew just enough to be an intelligent audience. He was an obvious enthusiast and she wondered again if she could recruit him; enthusiasm is infectious and he was an excellent speaker. She'd like him on her lecturing and tutoring staff. She tried not to think she was interested in him for a more personal reason.

They finished with cheese for him and fruit for her and then were invited back to their alcove for coffee. "That was a truly excellent meal," she told him. "Thank you for inviting me."

"You were impressed?"

"I was. I'm already wondering which client I should invite here for lunch. No one could resist signing a contract after a meal like that."

"You're all heart, Miss Gray. But it's nice to know that the meal has put you in the mood for saying yes."

"You're not selling services and I'm not a client. And you should know that I'm renowned for never saying yes unless I want to. Now excuse me a minute." She rose and went to the ladies' room.

If there was a test then the ladies' loo passed it. It was, of course, clean and well lit. There were thick towels, good quality soaps, seats in front of the mirrors. There was none of the tweeness that ruins so many places. She sat to freshen her make-up. There was a sparkle in her eyes that suggested she was enjoying herself.

*****

It was the kind of thing that happened, Jane suspected, more to women than to men. An evening could be ruined through no fault of their own. Surprisingly, she didn't see the warning signs at once.

When she returned, there was a party of men by the bar. She recognised their style instantly, local businessmen with the noisiness and arrogance that says small-town rich. They were about her age. As she walked across the room she could hear them being unpleasantly familiar with the barmaid, who was dealing with it professionally.

One of the four was enormous. He must have been about six feet three inches tall and weighed eighteen or nineteen stone. There were rolls of flesh round his neck and face but he still looked big rather than fat.

She had to cross behind the group to reach her alcove, she could just see the edge of the silver coffee tray. The four men were drunk enough to have lost their inhibitions.

It's something all women have to put up with at some time or other. As she passed, one of the four said "Have a drink with us, darling."

Jane shook her head and carried on walking. The man then mumbled something obviously crude to another, who laughed and stepped backward into her, causing her to stumble. He looked fuddled, too stupid to realise what he had done wrong.

The big man stepped forward. He was obviously used to being centre stage and the others looked at him with respect.

Surprisingly, his voice was high and squeaky. "Let me apologize for my friend's discourtesy. My name is Johnny Harris and I can't let you pass without some form of recompense. Let me buy you a drink."

"Thank you, no." Jane was polite but frigid.

"I really must insist, you know. You are the most delightful looking woman in the room."

He took hold of her wrist and she realised he was just as drunk as the others. He smiled. Good God, he imagined he was charming her.

So far no voices had been raised. But Alan had heard something and peered round the alcove corner, then quickly stood up. It was an odd thought to have at that moment, but she still contrasted his ease of movement with the lumbering shuffles of the four men around her. She shook her arm and snapped, "Please let me go." The big man did not release her. Still, it was a situation she'd been in before. She could cope with drunks.

She had to give Alan his due. He behaved perfectly. He faced the man and said flatly, "This lady is my guest. She does not want a drink with you. Let go of her arm."

Everything Mr Harris thought was immediately obvious. His face went red, showing he was not accustomed to being crossed. Younger, smaller men should be polite to people of his size and importance. He did not let go of Jane's wrist. "Run along, sonny, I'm not talking to you," he said.

Alan's shoulder drooped and jerked forward.

Something happened to the big man's face. His mouth opened in astonishment and tears squeezed from the corners of his eyes. He had an expression of vast disbelief, this couldn't be happening to him. He slumped forward.

Alan said to the other three men, "Your friend isn't feeling very well. Take him outside. In fact, taking him home would be a good idea."

Leaving their drinks, they led the fat man out. People looked at them curiously but stayed silent. The barmaid was industriously wiping glasses at the other end of the bar, she had carefully noticed nothing.

White-faced, Alan took Jane's arm and led her to their alcove. He was obviously very angry.

"What happened?" she asked. She must be tired. She still couldn't work it out.

"I hit him," Alan said evenly, "in what is called the solar plexus. It's a nerve centre."

She must have been in shock because her next words were magnificently tactless. "I haven't been out with anyone who hits people for over thirty years."

"A new experience for you. I do it all the time," he snarled.

For want of something to occupy her, she poured out their coffee. The manager suddenly appeared, wearing a concerned expression and carrying two brandies. The barmaid was better than Jane had thought, evidently she'd reported what had happened to the boss.

"I am so sorry for what has just occurred," said the manager. "Please accept these with our compliments. I do hope you haven't been too distressed and that we will see you again."

Jane smiled briefly. "We've thoroughly enjoyed the meal and I look forward to our next visit."

"Could I have the bill, please?" asked Alan and the manager retreated.

There was a tiny silence. "I hope we have time for me to finish my coffee?"

"Sure. Excuse me a minute."

He went to pay the bill rather than waiting for it to be brought to the table.

Jane sighed, reflecting on how easy it was to lose a mood.

When he returned, he had obviously decided to try to make the best of things. Forcing a smile, he said, "I don't think we can be comfortable here for much longer. Shall we go?"

There was a dispirited set to his shoulders as they crossed the courtyard. When they were back in the car Jane thought to herself that desperate problems required desperate solutions. So she leaned over, took his head between her hands and kissed him. It was meant to be a friendly, comforting act and she didn't expect the sudden rush of excitement that affected her in spite of herself. She pulled away hurriedly just as he became responsive.

"Thanks for the meal," she said quickly. "It was wonderful. Next time it's on me."

He reached toward her but she shook her head. "I only kiss people once in car parks. Can we have a look from Harper's Brow as we go home?"

He sucked in a vast chest-full of air then breathed out in a long soft sigh. "Of course," he said. "That will be good." She knew things would be all right.

As he drove out of the car park, Jane put on a CD of Handel's Messiah. "Music to digest to," she commented. The choir sang "Comfort ye."

"Chosen with taste," he said and the silence was so much less fraught.

It struck her that she was acting like a little mother again. In her time she had done a lot of it, lecturers could be temperamental. These days she didn't bother, she paid people enough to do without tantrums. On this occasion she was strangely happy to for once.

After fifteen minutes she directed him off the main road and they made for Harper's Brow -- a short stretch of road running along the edge of the hills fronting the coastal plain. There were car parks at regular intervals and he drove into one, fortunately unoccupied. They both got out and went to stand by the parapet, looking at the clusters of light that were towns and the lines of light that were main roads.

She took his wrist and felt for his pulse. "You're calming down," she said.

"A bit. I feel I acted like a lunatic in there. Brawling like a drunken rugby player. No better than them."

Carefully, she pointed out, "You were doing it to protect me."

"Was I? Or was I just trying to impress you? I suspect you could have handled the situation quite easily."

"Possibly," she admitted, "but I was grateful for your help."

She realised she was still holding his hand just as he realised the same. She gently released it. "It's been a long day," she said. "I think we'd better go back."

The silence on the way home was not tense; they were both at ease with the situation.

Outside her flat she said prosaically, "I'm not inviting you in, Alan. I've got business and I've got some thinking to do."

"Are you going to think about me?"

It was a naïve question but he wasn't a naïve man. "As a matter of fact I will think about you some of the time."

"Will I see you again soon?"

"I'll phone you in a couple of days. Let me say again, I did enjoy the meal and the company."

"So did I. I want to see more of you, Jane."

"Goodnight, Alan." She kissed him again, briefly, and although she knew he was tempted, he was bright enough not to turn the kiss into something that it was not. Then she went indoors.

Upstairs, undress, shower. There were messages on the answering machine and she dealt with them. Then it was time to think.

The decisions she had taken this afternoon were going to alter her life radically. Not only would she be rich, she'd be an internationalist, hopping from continent to continent. It was what she'd wanted, but with a thrill of horror she admitted that the events of the evening might have an ever greater impact on her. She was ... she was -- *interested* -- in Alan Murray.

Chapter Three

The next day was Sunday, traditionally a day of rest, so she stayed in bed an extra hour. Then she worked through from nine in the morning to nine at night. Walter G. Traekel had asked her for various details. He had said any time would do, but he was going to learn she did better than that.

Monday morning brought with it her normal work. Jane was determined to concentrate, but it was routine and she couldn't exclude stray thoughts as she had managed to do yesterday. Images of Alan's body, of the strength -- or character -- needed to hit someone five stone heavier flitted unbidden through her mind. She could do without this.

It was early but she phoned through to Kelly Colls, her personal trainer, and left a message on her machine that she'd like a session at lunchtime. She'd been partying too much.

She drove to her office. By choice this was not in the city centre. Instead she had a long lease on an old bank building in the expensive suburbs. It was easy to reach, easy to park, and there were excellent local hotels and restaurants used by her affluent neighbours. A good place for business.

Like her, Claude believed in arriving early for work. He was already working on his computer when she let herself in. "I'll fetch you a coffee," he said and followed her into her office carrying two cups.

One of the excellent things about Claude being gay was that they could talk with freedom about their personal lives. "Did you have a good evening on Saturday?" he asked.

"It should have been good. Alan took me to Harvey's Mill out on the moors. Have you been there? It's got good food and atmosphere, we could take favoured clients out there."

"So what went wrong?"

What had gone wrong? In retrospect it didn't seem any great deal. "There was a bit of unpleasantness at the bar," Jane said slowly. "A group of well-off local oafs were drunk. One of them was offensive, and Alan hit him -- very successfully, I'm afraid. He was quite upset afterwards."

"Ah. I sympathise."

She knew this was true. Being gay, Claude and Gavin suffered from more than their fair share of truculent bar-room louts.

"Are you going to see him again? You've been celibate for far too long."

She knew it was evading the issue to say that he hadn't asked her yet. She knew he would. So she merely answered, "I really don't know,

Claude. I've got plenty to occupy me at the moment."

"You've had plenty to occupy you as long as I've known you." They both sipped their coffee and he went on, "My grandmother used to say that you never accumulate unless you speculate. And that goes for relationships as well as finance."

"That's a very male point of view."

"Thank you, Jane. I'm flattered." He winked and they both laughed.

The cord from the blind was tied to its clip on the window edge and Claude pulled the end of it taut against the desk. Then he plucked it so it slapped against the leather top. "You're stretched too tight, Jane. If you don't relax soon, you'll snap." He released the cord which whipped back and rattled against the blind.

Irritated, she said, "That's a good party trick, a good illustration. I'll use it in my next lecture on stress."

"I already do," he said imperturbably.

She worked through her voice mail messages, faxes, e-mails, and letters. It was no secret that she did a good job and was a good organiser. To her it was simple. She decided what was most important and did it at once. She even gave lectures on the technique -- prioritising.

There was a letter from the Training Officer of Firmex Plastics, a large firm she had recently managed to sell courses to. She was pleased, it should turn into a set of lucrative long-term contracts. First she skimmed through the letter and then she read it through slowly, unable to cope with the rush of half-sick excitement that burst through her. It was perfect, one of those occasions when you're certain that you have a guardian angel looking especially after you. Then she thought again. One of the golden rules in her business was never to employ someone because you like her -- or him.

She asked Claude to come in, threw the letter at him, and said, "Read this, Claude, and then talk to me." It was a technique they both used when they needed to make a decision.

He read the letter carefully. "This is a firm we want to impress. They have written to us, asking us to find them someone to give a high-powered computer appreciation course for three days. They are sorry for the short notice, but their usual lecturer from the university is ill. Our own computer experts aren't quite up to this standard. You immediately think of Alan Murray, but are scared of the idea. You think personal feelings might cloud your judgement. I think there is a slight risk but I also think he'd do an excellent job. Ring him now."

"That's telling me. You don't think there's any special pleading on my part?"

"No." With a wicked grin Claude carried on, "We talked at some length on Saturday you know, Alan and I. I was already lining him up as a part-timer."

Jane felt a strange relief. "I'll phone him now. At work."

Everett Productions connected her to their computer section. It must have been a free and easy department, the man who answered the phone was obviously drinking coffee or something as he spoke. Jane thought that if she'd been in charge, she'd soon stop that. She asked for Alan Murray but before she could say who she was, the phone was put down and she heard a voice shout, "Young bit of totty for you, Alan."

Jane's lips tightened. She was not totty, young sounding or not.

She had to wait. Then, "Alan Murray here." A terse, pre-occupied voice, he was obviously not expecting her.

"Jane Gray. Is it a bad time to call? Are you busy?"

The alteration in tone was miraculous. "Jane! How good to hear from you. I was wondering after Saturday if you..."

"This is business, Alan," she interrupted. There was no way she was going to have any kind of intimate conversation on a line that ran through a switchboard. "If you're not busy, do you think you could call at my office on your way home tonight?"

He sounded puzzled. "Well, yes, I could." Then his voice warmed. "What I'd really like is..."

She cut him off again. "Do you know where my office is?"

"Well, yes I do. I looked up the address."

He was not sure of his reception now, his voice was wary so she decided to ease off a little. "It really is business, but perhaps we could have a drink afterward."

"Sounds good." He seemed more cheerful. "I can't be there until about seven. I've got a lot on here. Is that too late?"

"Seven is fine. Looking forward to it." She rang off, knowing she'd left him puzzled.

She shouted through to Claude, telling him Alan would call tonight. "I thought I had an adequate telephone manner," she added ruefully. "When I talk to him I feel like a teenage girl worried in case my boyfriend's father should hear us."

"Feel like a teenage girl?" Claude shouted back. "Lucky you."

Kelly e-mailed to confirm Jane's booking so at half past one she drove the two miles down to the little gym. There were regular lunchtime classes she could attend but she preferred to pay extra and have lessons to herself. She told Kelly she needed to work hard and they started a step aerobics routine with the usual pop music not too loudly in the background. She picked a high step and held silver dumbbells in her hands. Soon she had overcome her body's initial resistance and was in the mood. She was warm, breathing well, and feeling as if she could go on forever. Kelly reacted to her mood and pushed her harder than ever. Then eventually she stopped her.

"You're trying too hard to prove something, Jane. Not a good idea. We'll wind down now and then I think you should have a sauna."

Kelly was the expert, so Jane took her advice. When she got back to the office she felt wonderful.

*****

Alan arrived promptly at seven. Jane was alone in the building. Claude and the office staff had left. When she saw him walking across the car park she felt ludicrously like an adolescent again and she remembered an expression from those long gone school days. *He makes me feel squirmy.*

Squirmy? For heaven's sake she was a middle aged woman!

Alan looked just like a comic-book scientist, tweed jacket, grey flannels, checked shirt with university tie. She half expected to see a slide rule sticking out of his pocket. But her heart still beat a little faster.

When she unlocked the front door for him, his eyes flicked around her reasonably opulent reception area. The carpet was thick and there were large pot plants, impressive photographs, and a map of Europe with stickers indicating where she was running courses.

"Training is obviously one of our growth areas," he observed.

"It is. In the modern world it needs to be."

He was still wary so she decided to make things easy for him. "Alan, I never say anything personal or confidential on a work phone that goes through a switchboard. You might just as well publish in the company newspaper."

He thought a minute. "Is that why you were so chillingly formal this afternoon?"

"It certainly is. A lesson I learned painfully -- oh, years ago."

"I see. I hadn't thought of that." She could tell he was thinking of it now.

He was starting to relax so she went on, "Come upstairs to my office. I've got coffee on."

"There's a pub just up the road, what about a drink there?"

Obviously he wanted to meet her on what might be called neutral ground, so she said, "I'll make you an offer. Business until half past eight and then some time for pleasure."

"Pleasure?" he queried. "That sounds fun." She felt gently warm.

When they were seated in her office she gave him the specifications of the course that was required -- without giving him the name of the firm -- and asked if he could design a course that covered it and that he could teach to intelligent, reasonably computer-literate managers over three Sundays.

He scanned the page. "May I borrow your machine? I think better in front of a screen." Before she realised what was happening she was being bundled out of her seat behind the desk and he was sitting sideways, looking at her terminal. Suddenly, Jane saw a new side of him. This man was efficient!

Her office computer system cost her a great deal. As his fingers flicked over the keyboard, like a pianist playing Bach, she said, "I've been very pleased with this system. It's saved me an awful lot of time and work."

"It's all right. Good enough for what you want, but it's a bit old-hat."

"I only bought it a year ago!"

"I guessed that. Like I said, old-hat. Computing science updates itself at least every twelve months." He frowned at the figures in front of him. "I like my coffee quite strong. White, but with no sugar please."

She had been dismissed. It was her own fault for allowing him to sit in front of the computer. Now he was king and he'd pay attention to her when he felt like it. *Well really, Jane,* she scolded herself, *if you ask an expert his opinion, you have to put up with the result.* She fetched his coffee.

There was no reason to bother. When she put the mug on the desk in front of him, he mumbled something, and pushed it to one side. So she drank her coffee and watched him. He referred to the specifications of the course, tapped in a few paragraphs, paused, and lifted his eyes vacantly, apparently praying to the great god of electronic communications. Then he typed some more. Eventually he read through what he'd written, made a couple of alterations and printed it. Only then did he reach for his lukewarm coffee.

"This is a course outline that you could submit and there are a few notes on what I'd actually teach. I'll need more time to develop these. Before teaching any of this I would want a briefing session with the people involved and a quick look at the hardware and software available. I could do the course in three days but four days would be better."

"How do you feel about teaching high level managers?"

"Teaching computing? Very happy. I've taught some post-graduate work at the university, you know."

She hadn't known -- and should have asked. His confidence was justified then, as well as her own gut instinct. He'd be a good tutor.

She looked through what he had written and was impressed. It was a very clear course outline. She move into formal mode and made him an offer. "I'll submit this to the client firm for their approval but I'm sure they'll accept it. Jane Gray Associates has certain protocols -- standards and definite ways of working. Claude will go through them with you later. But provisionally we'll offer you a contract for expenses and seven hundred pounds a day."

"I accept."

She noticed he didn't query the amount. He obviously knew he was worth it. He grinned at her. "Have we got the business over? Can we go for that drink now?"

Alan's confidence had returned. Jane felt affection for him welling inside her. "Yes, business is over, but I'm going to cheat and take you for a meal and charge it to expenses. It's not every day I sign a new lecturer."

He frowned. "Just one thing. I'm supposed to clear any extra work I do with the management of Everett Products, but they did say when I started that they encouraged their staff to take on odd teaching jobs to help develop local talent."

"I'll have a word with Howard Metcalfe," promised Jane, and tried not to show how tough she expected that word would be. Howard was not going to be pleased with her.

She set the alarm system, locked up, and they walked across the road to the Kelton Arms. She was well-known there. Although they were not officially serving food, she asked the manager if he could arrange a couple of steak sandwiches for them and since she was a valued customer he said yes. She ordered beer for Alan and a white wine for herself on the company account.

"I thought we'd stopped being employer and employee," he said.

"We certainly have. Now I'm just Jane -- which is just as well because sometimes you're definitely Tarzan -- big, strong, and king of the bar-room jungle."

He looked mortified. "Come on, Jane. Do I have to suffer this each time we meet?"

She smiled. "I'll tell you a secret if you promise to keep it. I'm having difficulty in admitting it to myself, but I quite liked being fought over. It made me feel all cave-womanish."

He looked at her mournfully. "Miss Gray, the perfidy of women. I thought you were the soul of propriety. You'll have me old before my time."

"Oh, I do hope not."

The steak sandwiches arrived, and as they ate they talked, a gentle non-pressured conversation, casual but not aimless. They were getting to know each other. He told her how he broke his nose on a rugby tour of Ireland and how he no longer played for the first team. She felt a touch of proprietary relief. She told him how she first met Claude and what a help he had been to her and how funny he and Gavin were the way they argued all the time but couldn't live apart. They had another drink and talked some more. Time was passing agreeably.

Jane glanced at her watch as he suggested a third round. It was half past nine. "Sorry, Alan, but it's time I went back to work. Besides, I can't encourage you to drink and drive."

Since she stood up he had to do the same. They walked toward the door and he said, "D'you know, the word 'work' occurs every time we meet."

"My work is my life," she said simply. "It's what makes me who I am."

"There has to be more to life than work!"

"Perhaps for other people." They walked back across the road to their parked cars. What he had just said might be true but she had no time to think about it now.

As they reached their cars, he turned to her and said harshly, "It's only half past nine and I don't want the evening to end. If you're so worried about drink driving, then we could have a drink somewhere near your flat and I could go home on the last train again." He said nothing more as Jane looked at him, made no attempt to touch or convince her.

Jane was silent. His sudden request had turned this meeting into a confrontation and she was not ready for one yet. "What do you want of me, Alan?" she asked.

His reply was slow and thoughtful. "I don't know, but I know there's something more. You know as much, or as little, as I do."

More minutes passed and then she said, "Drive to the station car park at Clennan. If I'm not there in half an hour then drive home."

It wasn't hard to see his desperate urge to say something -- but wisely he conquered it. "All right." He got in his car and drove off.

She sat in her car. She stroked the wooden dashboard, smelled the leather upholstery. Behind her was her office block with her name on the panel outside. If she wriggled in her seat she could feel the caress of silk underwear. She was well-off, happy, successful, fulfilled, healthy. What more could she want? She could certainly do without the sticky emotional mess of having a lover. If she did have an affair it would be something proper and discreet, with someone near her own age. Alan Murray was not for her.

She was almost home when she heaved the steering wheel round and U-turned back to the station. Why, she was not sure. She pulled in beside Alan's car. He got out and she said, "Leave your car here. We'll go back to my place."

He locked his car, and slid into her passenger seat. As she reached for the lever to notch into reverse, he covered her hand with his and held it fast. "You're making all the decisions, Jane. I'm just doing what I'm told."

"Too right I'm making all the decisions. And let me tell you, they're difficult." Then after a moment, she said, "I lied. I'm not making decisions. I just can't help myself. This has never happened to me before. What are you doing to me?"

He leaned over to kiss her gently on the cheek. "I just want to be with you."

*****

Back at her flat, Jane clicked on the side lights in the living room. This was the second time she'd brought him back in the evening, could it get to be a habit? She turned restlessly, but before she could say anything

Alan led her to the couch.

He said, "Jane, it's ten o'clock. What time did you start work this morning?"

She told him.

"How long did you work for yesterday?"

"Twelve hours."

"On a Sunday. I already know you flew to London the day before."

"I had a man to see."

"When I met you at the party, what had you done that day?"

"Alan, I never stop working. If I don't work at least a ten hour day, I think I'm slacking. Work is my life. I love it, just like you do."

He let go of one of her hands and ran his finger down the side of her face. She couldn't think of anyone else she would permit to touch her in this fashion but she let Alan. He said, "There's a muscle here at the side of your mouth that's tight all the time. Only when you smile does it relax and then you look lovely. But you don't smile enough."

For a minute she was content to sit there as he held her hand and caressed her. She didn't care to consider his analysis at the moment. Then, almost hysterically, she jumped to her feet and said," I seem to have been in this suit forever, I'm going to change. There's a bottle of white wine in the fridge, get a couple of glasses and help yourself. Make yourself comfortable, take off your coat. I'll be right back."

He listened to this gabbled set of instructions and said nothing as she escaped to her bedroom.

Showering had a calming effect on her. As the water ran down her naked body, she made a decision of sorts. She decided *not* to decide. For this evening, she would simply let things happen. She remembered the old sixties expression *Go with the flow*. This was entirely unlike her but she felt liberated. And then, with an almost physical shock, she realised what she did want. She wanted Alan Murray.

After she'd towelled herself dry, she opened her underwear drawer -- then shut it. There was the red velour tracksuit she wore when she worked around the house, she ignored that too. Instead she put on a black silk kimono embroidered with fire-breathing dragons. Claude brought it back for her from Hong-Kong. The silk felt good against her skin.

She was tense again as she walked into the living room. Alan sat there peacefully. He said, "That's a nice gown." He'd put the Goldberg Variations on to play softly in the background and she wondered how he could match her mood so exactly.

She sat by him and he poured her a glass of wine -- one of her best Saumurs. The sea was beating in the distance, she felt it rather than heard it. "I don't want to get too drunk," she said and he put a friendly arm round her shoulders.

Her body seemed to be sensitised, as she lifted the glass to her lips she felt as if everything she perceived had a new intensity. Across the wrinkled sea, she could see a ship's lights, they seemed important. She could feel the stroke of silk against her body, hear the iron-gripped passion of the Klavier music. The wine smelled of honeysuckle and had the spiky taste of lemons and green apples.

His arm was comforting against her shoulders so she leaned back against it. It was warm and muscular. There was the feeling that they had all the time in the world and that they fitted well together. She sipped again and then put down her glass. He did the same.

Entirely at her ease she sat still as he turned and kissed her. First there was the soft kiss on the lips, unhurried and undemanding. She glanced at those brilliant green eyes then closed her own. He moved and kissed her cheeks, her forehead, touched with his tongue that tender spot at the edge of her eye. His breath was warm with the sharp taste of wine to it. As he moved his head away a little she knew that he was looking at her.

Again she remembered that schoolgirl expression. She felt all squirmy -- but never then as she did now. She felt as if she was about to live in a different way and she was a bit afraid.

When he rested his cheek against hers, her senses flamed at the faint abrasion of his beard. "Your skin is rough," she whispered.

Equally softly he replied, "I'm sorry but I haven't had chance to shave since this morning and I..."

Leaning forward she kissed him briefly on the lips. "Hush, I like it." It was true, she did. She wrapped her arms round his shoulders.

He kissed her on the lips, a little harder this time and she felt the tentative probing of his tongue. The next step would be irretrievable, but her lips parted of their own accord. She trembled, knowing this was a symbol, foreshadowing another, greater surrender. For a moment he leaned over her, crushing her against him. She could sense passion, urgency, the sheer need of youth. Then, with steely self-control, he leaned back against the couch again. One arm was around her, with his free hand he traced gentle lines over her face as he did before. "You're beautiful," he said. His voice was rough, out of control, and she thought the simple compliment was the most heartfelt she'd ever heard.

"You're good to me," she said and waited for what he would do next. She took a last look at his wonderful mouth and the now heavy-lidded green eyes, and closed her eyes. Cutting off one sense enhanced the others, his fingers felt like magic as once again they stroked the curves of her forehead, cheekbones, bottom lip. Then, after the slightest of pauses, they tracked down the side of her throat where the pulse beat. Then into the vee where her kimono was wrapped around her.

He leaned over to kiss her, gently this time and then his hand eased aside the silk and his finger tips stroked the swell of her breasts.

Her pulse quickened again, her breathing was more rapid. She sighed at the most exquisite of feelings and realised it was her nipples coming erect and rubbing against the silk. His hand now stroked and caressed, pulling the kimono away. She clutched at his forearms, not to stop him, but because she had to hold him somehow. His head bent again, but this time not to her lips and she cried out as his tongue touched and then his mouth enfolded each breast in turn.

So far she had done little, bewildered by her body's needs. She needed to do something, even if it was just a sign of her acceptance. So she took the knotted cord of her kimono and pulled it apart. As the kimono opened she heard his sudden deep breath. She stood, turned to face him and took his hands in hers. As she bent over to do so her kimono fell further open and she felt her breasts surge forward. She didn't care as she saw the passion flare in his eyes. "We're uncomfortable here," she said. "Come to bed."

"Jane, are you sure?"

She put her finger on his lips and led him from the room.

*****

The bedside lights were on, the room was dim. He hadn't been in her bedroom before and his eyes swept round as if not knowing what to expect.

She wondered what he saw, what it told him about her. It was neat, of course, and not overly feminine. The built-in units were in light wood, the carpet not long and woolly but a rich dark Axminster. There were two prints of eighteenth century landscapes. Her bed was a double.

Suddenly she felt a flash -- not of panic but apprehension. She didn't want him to be disappointed. Not in her, perhaps, but because of his own inexperience. He was so much younger than her. To quell any doubts he might have -- and any that she might have -- she reached up to kiss him. They had come so far, they mustn't, daren't go back. She felt the passion in his body. "I want you undressed," she said.

He led her to her own bed and they stood facing each other. Jane saw desire in his eyes, but also a wonderful something else that she didn't want to name.

With a strength she'd only guessed at, he held her under her arms and lifted her effortlessly upward. Her feet were off the ground, she was helpless but she didn't care. Then he lowered her gently onto the bed. "Lie there," he said. She shut her eyes, putting her hands behind her head. She heard the rustling of clothing.

He pushed the kimono away so he could see all of her. "Jane, oh Jane," he breathed in an almost reverent voice. But she was still constricted so she pulled her arms out of the sleeves and wriggled out of the kimono. Now she was truly naked, below him. A thrill shook her as he lowered his body onto hers.

He was sweet and considerate but he was young and not very experienced. He wanted to do all he could for her and his hands roamed her body, making her pant and sigh. She could feel his urgency and she was happy to go along with it, so soon, all was over. He called her name, half groaned, half sighed, and she felt him surge on top of her. Then he lay there with his face on the curve of her shoulder and she stroked his back. He was lovely.

Though there was something in her perhaps still unsatisfied, she felt contentment with him there. It was better to give than to take. He lifted his head so their faces were inches apart, and smiled. "Jane Gray, I feel guilty because I was selfish, but I also feel very happy. You're gorgeous and next time will be even better."

Next time? Jane felt as if a net was being pulled around her-- but she didn't want to escape it.

"You're a wonderful lover," she said, and meant it.

"Does that mean you love me?" he asked.

She couldn't answer.

Chapter Four

Jane woke even earlier than usual but she didn't get out of bed. All through the night she had slept on her side with her back to Alan, his arm wrapped round her, his hand gently holding her breasts. It had been magical. It had made her feel how lonely a single person in a double bed could be. But now she needed to stop feeling and start to think. What happened last night and through the night had been pure bliss. Now she had to decide what would come next.

As soon as she tried to slide out of bed, he reached for her and pulled her to him. She couldn't help herself, she had to give in. He kissed her cheek, then her shoulder but she realised he was only half awake. Still, their bodies were pressed together, it was hard to ease herself away from him. Sadly, there were things she had to do.

"It's early," she said. "Lie there till I come back."

"If it's early then we can..."

"Shhh. Just lie still and I'll be back."

He was a sensitive man, he recognised this was not the time to argue. "I'm not going anywhere," he sighed, took his arms from around her waist, shook his head, and dropped back onto the pillow. She felt bad but...

It only took twenty minutes to shower, dress, and percolate the coffee. Then she poured two mugs and carried them to bed.

He said, "Coffee? Sweetheart, I want to..."

He was awake enough to understand her message but she knew he wouldn't like it. "I'm sorry, Alan, but I've got to get to work and so do you. You've got half an hour to drink your coffee, wash, and dress then I'll drop you off by your car."

"But I thought we might..."

"I can guess what you thought. Alan, it just isn't going to happen. Last night was last night; it was marvellous. This morning we have to get back into the real world."

"At this moment I don't think much of the real world. All I can think about is spending all my time with you."

"Alan, drink your nice coffee then get into the bathroom. I've put a towel ready for you. We leave in thirty minutes."

He didn't like it but he was bright enough to know that she wasn't kidding. "I'll be ready in twenty-five minutes," he said. He swallowed a mouthful of hot coffee and winced. She went to check her bag.

He had accepted the situation and was nearly his old self as they left the flat. Only ten minutes to drive him to where he had left his car in the station car park.

There was a message she had to get across in those ten minutes. She knew he wouldn't like this one either.

As they went down in the lift he tried to kiss her. She turned her head so he could only brush his lips against her cheek. "Real world, remember? We have to behave."

"I think we can make our own real world and behave as we wish."

"Life isn't that simple."

He thought about this as they entered the garage and she negotiated her way out onto the road. Then she tried to say what had to be said. It was difficult.

"Alan, last night was wonderful and I don't regret a minute of it, but it can't go on. I think you're a lovely person and I hope we can continue being friends, but that must be all."

His reply was sharp. "Is that all last night was? A one-night stand? A pick up and two dates later we fetch up in bed? Wave a cheerful goodbye to each other next morning, nice to have met you, perhaps we'll do it again some time?"

The bitterness in his voice made Jane understand even more what he was suffering. He hadn't yet acquired her skill in concealing feelings. His words hurt her deeply because his accusation had some truth in it. It would be foolish to let him know her pain too. She would have to be a touch brutal. "Be reasonable, Alan. First, I'm not in the least interested in an affair that will peter out in a few weeks. Been there, done that, it hurt. Also, I don't like to think what it would do for my professional reputation, being seen regularly with you and then suddenly not at all. I'd be a laughing stock."

"One; who says what we have will peter out? Two; who cares about reputation?"

"Why should what we have peter out? One stark fact. I'm much older than you. As for reputation, I care because reputation is all I've got. My firm survives on it. I've worked for years developing it and I'm not going to throw it away."

Surprisingly, he accepted this. "All right, I take your points about age and reputation, but I don't think they're insurmountable. People bring me so-called unsolvable problems and I sort them out on the computer. There will be a way, Jane."

"Feelings can't be programmed."

He sighed. "You're telling me. Tell me more about this affair that hurt you so much. Is that what made you such an ice-maiden?"

She was shocked -- and cross with herself. She'd forgotten how alert he could be and she had let something slip. She tried to steer him away from the subject. "You, if anyone, should know I'm not an ice-maiden." She glanced at him and saw him smile to himself.

"Quite so. Jane, I think you are wonderful and I..."

She was saved. The ten minutes were up. She swung into the station car park and pulled up beside his car. She leaned over, kissed him on the cheek and said, "Time to part and we..."

She hadn't realised how assertive he could be. It was a side of his character that had not yet fully come out, but as she now discovered, it was certainly there. He spoke like a man who was neither expecting nor willing to accept a contradiction. "No. You know as well as I do we've started something which can't be finished in a station car park. We've things to decide, to sort out. I'd like to be invited back to your flat but if you wish we'll meet in a pub or go for a drive in the country. Jane, we have to talk. You owe that to me. More importantly, I think you owe it to yourself."

Now that was a subtle point. She supposed what he said was true. "All right. Anyway, I'll need to talk to you about this lecturing you're to do for me. I'll ring you to arrange..."

He took a card from his pocket gave it to me. "Ring me on my private mobile. I'm particular about the number though, don't give it away. Only a handful of people know it." He opened the car door then leaned over to kiss her briefly on the lips. "It would be nice if you could call tonight ... just to arrange a time and place. Even if it was just to say hello, or goodnight, I'd like it. Bye, sweetheart."

He opened the door of his own car. She drove off at once.

*****

It was early, the building was quiet, there was no one working except the cleaning staff. She walked to her comfortable office. This was her little kingdom where she felt she was truly herself. No Claude, he was running a course today. She felt a bit sorry, she would have liked a chat.

For an hour she lost herself in work, the usual shoal of phone messages, letters, e-mails, reports. Then she realised what she was doing. She was putting off thinking. This wasn't like her, she always faced up to challenges.

She checked her pulse -- a bit too high. So she reclined her chair, put her feet on a drawer pulled out of her desk, and closed her eyes. After ten minutes she felt rejuvenated.

She fetched a glass of iced water from the office fridge and when she returned there was a cartoon figure dancing on her computer screen. It was a big man in a bathing costume. As he danced great muscles appeared on his biceps, his chest, his thighs -- and they were dancing too. She looked at it in amazement -- it was like nothing she had seen before. Then suddenly there was music. A voice sang, "I've got you under my skin." The figure pointed downwards so she scrolled down. The music changed to "...make me feel so good," and there was a message.

> *Words have failed me so I'm trying music. Please reply to this message, rating it from one to ten in which ten represents maximum pleasure.*

Right. It was a clever idea and she didn't know how he had done it but there were limits. She was wary of anything personal coming through on a computer. She pressed return and typed, *None out of ten. Furthermore, anyone found messing with my computing system will regret it.*

Then she deleted the dancing man, although she had liked him quite a lot.

She stared at the screen. She knew that Alan would have to respond. Five minutes later there was the cartoon figure again, but this time the music was Heartbreak Hotel and tears were streaming from his eyes. The message read, *So sorry. Forgive me?*

She typed in, *Just this once. Never again.* Then she pressed send. She realised this was the kind of exchange she would have loved twenty years ago. Was she losing her sense of humour as she got older?

To work. Her staff had now arrived and there were the usual assorted problems to deal with. Two things kept niggling at her. Two things Alan had said. One, he had asked her about the affair that had turned her into an ice maiden. Two, he had said that she owed it to herself to decide just what he meant to her.

It was not a decision that could be put off.

Her brain now needed all the stimulus it could get so she fetched herself a cup of coffee. The office coffee machine cost a fortune, but it was worth it. She sipped her espresso and stared out of the window. There was nothing but sky to see and the occasional lost seagull. She couldn't deal with Alan now, her mind had been jerked back to when ... Good Lord, when he was five. For a self-indulgent second Jane tried to imagine him in short trousers and ... forget that! Other, more powerful, images were surging through her brain.

She didn't think of that time as often as she used to. The lessons she had learned were seared into her brain. Perhaps they'd helped her become successful. She wouldn't be unique in that.

It had started, of course, with a man. Lawrence Holmes. He hadn't liked being called Larry, he thought it diminished him, he was not a child. He was a good looking man, almost pretty in fact. He took a lot of care over his appearance, had more expensive cosmetics than she had. He was never seen less than perfectly dressed, spent vast sums on his wardrobe. She'd thought he was wonderful.

She had just left university at the time and was taking a one year post-graduate course in management. It was hard, but she liked hard work. There were fifteen of them in the class, she was the only woman.

Apart from her, all the students were mature, most had been sent and were financed by their firms. But they all got on.

Lawrence had come from Australia for the course. He sat next to her in the inaugural meeting and they got talking and then went for a drink. He was years older than her and she thought he was intensely sophisticated. He made her laugh with his stories about life in the outback and how it was hard out there to find a good-looking woman to talk to. He was going to move to Adelaide when he returned, his firm had promised him this. Adelaide was full of attractive women. Like her.

Not an uncommon story. He was good looking and good company. She was bright, probably brighter than him, but she'd spent most of her university life studying. She wanted to get on. All right, she was naïve and gullible, which explained how she was persuaded to move into his flat some weeks later. Persuaded? She wanted to. She was in love, or so she thought.

And there were some happy times. Lawrence was always good for a laugh. But often they were laughing when they should have been working. He didn't have the same attitude to work that she had, often she had to help him write his essays, help him prepare his talks. She didn't mind. She loved him.

All the students had to write a thesis, based on observations. Lawrence and Jane agreed to help each other, first they'd do his then they'd work on hers.

Just thinking about those days angered her. How could she have been such a fool? She even agreed to pay her half of the rent -- and did all the cooking and cleaning.

Then, one morning two months before their final exams, she was working on the settee while Lawrence was showering. He'd just bought himself one of the then new-fangled portable phones. He was very proud of it. She couldn't afford one. His phone rang. She picked it up and said "Hello."

A female voice with an Australian accent asked, "Oh, I thought this was Lawrence Holmes's phone number."

"It is. He's having a shower. Shall I call him?"

"In a minute. First, who are you?"

Not a very pleasant tone but Jane answered politely. "My name's Jane Gray. I'm a friend of his."

"A friend? How close a friend?" The tone had got worse.

"I'm sorry, who is calling?"

For a moment she had forgotten one of the basic rules of management: never start a conversation with anyone on the telephone until they had identified themselves to your satisfaction.

Now the woman did identify herself. "You just knock on the bathroom door and tell Lawrence that his wife wants a word. Tell him I've just arrived in London."

"Wife? Lawrence isn't married."

"Is that what he told you? The ring on my finger tells me different. So would his two children."

Jane thought this must be a mistake. Someone playing a nasty joke, maybe. There was a sick feeling in her throat as she knocked on the bathroom door and shouted for Lawrence to come out at once, he was needed badly.

He opened the door with a towel wrapped round his waist and said "I'm still having my shower, what is it that can't wait until..."

"There's a woman on the phone who says she's your wife," said Jane. When she saw his face, she knew it was no mistake.

*****

She had moved out of the flat that very morning and told him she never wanted to speak to him again. Worse was to come. It turned out that much of the work she had done on her thesis he'd entered as his own work with his tutor. There was little to prove him a liar.

That was the moment Jane became the hard businesswoman she now was. She wept for the whole of one afternoon. Then she vowed she'd never act so stupidly again, and she hadn't.

There was one big difference between Lawrence and her. She could work, he could not. There were two months until the exams, she could catch up. All she needed was to eat and sleep a little, the rest of the time she would study. She studied. She lost nearly a stone, but as she sat the exams she knew she'd caught up on the work. It was so much easier without having to worry about Lawrence. For the first time in two months she spoke to him. "I've done well," she said. "I'll get a good pass. I've done the work, I know I have. How about you, Lawrence?"

Lawrence had failed. He was offered the chance to re-sit. He didn't take it.

Now, so many years later, Jane asked herself whether Alan was any better than Lawrence. Yes, she knew he was. She had learned over the past eighteen years, she could judge character now. She had no worries about Alan being a cheat.

Did she want to change from being the woman she had made herself? She'd got by without needing excessive emotions, but she suspected Alan wouldn't settle for a casual relationship. She was happy though. Why should she change now?

She thought about it on and off all through the morning. Finally, of all things, Shakespeare came to her aid. A half-forgotten quotation from Macbeth, studied in school. *T'were well if it were done quickly.* She conveniently overlooked the fact that what Macbeth was doing would seal his fate and lead to his ultimate death. She wanted a happier conclusion when she had done quickly. All she was going to do was agree to meet him.

Sometimes circumstances conspired to ease you into a decision you'd already half made. Like now. An e-mail appeared on Jane's screen from Firmex Plastics. They liked the proposals for an intensive IT course and were willing to arrange for it to last for four days. Would she get in touch with their Human Resources Department to discuss details? Claude could do that, thought Jane. But there was one thing she must do herself -- square everything with Howard Metcalfe.

It was now late morning. She rang Howard's secretary and yes, she could see him any time in the next two hours if it was only for a few minutes. What will the meeting be about? She said she'd explain when she got there.

It was only a half hour's drive to Everett Products. She was shown straight into his office and Howard eyed her thoughtfully. "You didn't want to tell my secretary why you wanted to see me," he said. "That worries me, Jane. Whatever it is, it's not going to be good news."

"That depends," she said, and cut straight to the chase. "I want to use Alan Murray as a lecturer on a high level course for four Sundays. Apparently he needs your permission. He wanted to ask you himself, but I told him I'd do it. Less embarrassment all round."

"I see. I did warn you about trying to poach him. What happens if I say no?"

She shrugged. "I'm not poaching him, Howard, I'm offering him extra work. You have the right to veto it. He won't do the job. You are a valued customer and I hope our relationship will continue."

"Which firm is it for?"

Usually she refused to answer that kind of question. She tried to guarantee discretion. Things were different on this occasion. "Firmex Plastics. There'll be no danger of Alan letting slip any kind of useful information. Incidentally, he might benefit by seeing the workings of an even larger organisation than this."

"True." Howard stared at her silently for a minute and then said, "Okay, I give my permission. I didn't realise you were talking to Alan that intensively at the party."

"I gave him a lift."

"And since then?"

Now she was wary. Where was Howard going? "We've met a couple of times. To talk about computing, the work he could do for me."

"Is that all? There's nothing ... personal between you?"

"Howard! That's not the sort of thing that can be asked." Jane was even more wary now.

"I know. Business is business, but you know as well as I do how difficulties in personal relationships in a firm can cause no end of trouble. I've had very good employees leave very good jobs because they couldn't stand working with particular people, for instance. It's a waste."

"Howard, you know me. I don't cause that kind of trouble."

"I hope not. Jane, we work well together, we like each other. You know I'm thinking as much about you as I am about the firm?"

"I know," she said. "You can rely on me to be careful."

"Good. You may borrow Alan, but don't steal him." Howard stood and reached from behind his desk to shake her hand. It was obviously time for her to leave.

*****

Back in the office, Jane phoned Alan on his mobile. It took quite a while for him to answer. "Alan Murray here."

She loved the sound of his voice. "Alan, it's Jane, I've got news for you."

"Great to hear from you, Jane, but I can't talk now. Got a problem that has to be sorted! Can I ring you back in an hour?"

"No problem. I'll be in my office all afternoon." She rang off. She liked it when he was professional.

She worked in the office but she found herself watching the clock, the hour seemed to be progressing very slowly. Eventually -- as he had said, exactly an hour later -- he rang. His voice was rushed, excited. "Hi, Jane, sorry about earlier, wanted to talk to you but some idiot in one of our other branches caused a problem with our supply lines and I had to..."

"It doesn't matter. You wouldn't be the man I think you are if you took time off an important job to talk to some woman or other."

"You are not some woman or other to me!" Then his voice eased, "As you very well know. You're making fun of me."

"Possibly," she agreed. "Alan, this is about work. I've got Howard's permission, if not his blessing, for you to give those lectures."

"Good. We'll have to work together. I'm looking forward to it already."

"A lot of the time you'll be working with Claude. We'll fix up a meeting. First I think there's something we have to sort out between the two of us. You were right this morning, we owe it to each other."

"I'm glad you think that," he said quietly. "I've been worried in case I'd been a bit ... well, pushy. Now I'll be businesslike. I've got a programme running tomorrow that'll take all day. It'll not finish till ten at night and by that time I'll be incapable of rational thought. But I'll be entitled to time off in lieu. I could meet you any time the rest of the week. Wednesday?"

Jane flicked open her diary. This was better than she could have planned.

"Wednesday afternoon would be good. I've got to go out to inspect a hotel. Occasionally I run weekend residential courses, finding a suitable venue isn't easy. You can come with me and give me your opinion."

"Time with you will be good, even if it still sounds a bit like work."

"I never stop working. I'll take you to dinner afterward and we can have a talk. One thing, Alan, wonderful though it might have been, no way we are repeating last night."

"Never?"

"A man can dream. Be at my office at two on Wednesday." She rang off.

It was an interesting journey to the hotel with Alan and Jane wondered if Howard had had some kind of word with him. Perhaps Alan was more people-aware than she had thought. He was obviously pleased to see her but he didn't try to kiss her when they met. He was happy to be driven in her car. He was wearing a suit that was sober and suitably business-like. As they drove to the hotel he didn't talk about anything personal, didn't mention their night together. Instead he questioned her about what she was looking for. What did she want from the place? What did delegates look for? How could she tell what is right and what is wrong?

She explained to him the importance of being close to rail and motorway links. That they would need at least fifty en-suite bedrooms, a main lecture theatre, and a number of break-out rooms. A bar was essential. She had looked at specimen menus and was happy with them.

"You've told me about everything but price," he said after a while. "Isn't that important? Howard wants costs for everything."

"You never look at price first, you look for quality. Anyway, nearly all of our delegates are paid for by their firms. We don't want them leaving thinking they've had a good cheap time. We want people leaving thinking that they've learned something -- and they'll come back to learn more."

His questions were well-thought out, he had a business mind. It struck her that he'd be a real asset as a full time member of her firm. Not, however, while she was selling so much to Howard Metcalfe.

Russell Manor had just been extensively refurbished and as they moved up the drive she thought it could be just the thing she needed. It was a handsome Georgian building in red stone. The gardens were well presented and there was more than ample parking space

She had phoned to arrange their visit, stated the time when she expected to arrive, and as she pulled up by the front doors someone came out to meet them. "Good afternoon, Miss Gray, I am John Mellows, the hotel manager. Welcome to Russell Manor."

This was good. It suggested that this was a place, where they were eager to please customers. They would take that all-important extra step.

It took two hours to look round, for Mr Mellows to answer all her questions, but at the end of that time she was impressed. It was as good as stated. They had been introduced to some of the staff and she could tell they were as enthusiastic as their manager.

"I'll be in touch, Mr Mellows," she said as they left. "I think we'll be doing business with you."

"It'll be a pleasure."

"Any comments, Alan?" she asked as they drove out onto the main road.

"I don't know much about the hotel business, but like you, I was impressed. It was good that all the bedrooms had free wifi as well as the main rooms. I had a quick squint at his office computers, all top of the range." His voice changed. "Now, I think I've been good so far. Can we stop being business people and just be me and you?"

Jane chuckled. "Fair enough. I must say you have been very good. Yes, we can be me and you."

"Great!" He leaned over to kiss her gently on the cheek. "So where are we going now?"

In fact they drove back to the office so Jane could write up her report on the hotel. It was too early to go for an evening meal. Claude was at the office, having had a successful day lecturing. Jane left Alan chatting to him in the staff lounge while she worked.

Then she went to the cloakroom to change. She'd had to be business-smart when she visited the hotel, she'd worn a dark blue trouser suit. For the evening she had decided to wear something a touch more feminine and brought along a little black dress. She had four little black dresses in various styles, she liked them.

When she finally got to the staff lounge she found Claude and Alan deep in conversation. As far as she could make out they were trying to decide whether, in twenty years or so, every person in the country would have a personal computing system fixed directly to their brain. This was not something she wished to consider.

"I'm taking Alan to the Creston Arms for a meal," she told Claude. "Like to come and join us?" She deliberately avoided looking at Alan.

"It's a tempting offer," Claude said genially. "But after seeing the look of sheer horror on Alan's face, I think I'll decline. Goodnight to you both. Enjoy your meal." And he was gone.

There was silence in the room for a moment. Then Alan said, "Asking Claude to join us was a joke, wasn't it?"

Jane walked over to kiss him on his cheek. "Yes, of course. I do have a sense of humour, Alan."

"I know. Sometimes it scares me."

"Let's go and eat. I've reserved a table."

*****

The Creston Arms wasn't as smart as Harvey's Mill. She was not trying to impress Alan as she suspected he had been trying to impress her. It was near the centre of town, was wildly popular with business people at lunchtime, but was quieter and had a different clientele at night. There was no large central area. Instead there were a set of intimate corners, where in the middle of the day businessmen could huddle together and plot -- or at night, where lovers could whisper to each other.

They were led to a suitable table. They sat on a banquette, side by side. They decided that they both wanted salad and would share a bottle of house white wine. By unspoken agreement they spoke of nothing of importance until they had finished eating and were drinking their second glass of wine. Then they could talk.

"I'm going to tell you how I feel," said Alan directly. "First of all, sex with you was fantastic, but that's not why I feel the way I do. I've never been attracted to someone so quickly before and never to someone like you. It's ... exciting and also it's a bit scary. I'm finding it hard to cope. Please don't patronize me and tell me you're old and I'm young and this makes a relationship impossible and that I'll get over it."

"That's honest." she said after thinking for a moment. "I like you for it. Did saying it hurt?"

"Quite a bit." He smiled. "I'm glad you said you liked me. Is that a start?"

"If it is, I don't know what we're starting. Alan, we barely know each other. We've met three times in a week. I have no idea of your history, your family, even your politics. All I do know is that you're a very attractive young man with an excellent mind. All you know is that I'm a successful, well-to-do business woman who is also attractive and much older than you."

"You didn't act much older on Saturday night!"

She winced. She felt angry, partly because it was true, partly because ... because she wasn't in control? Now that *was* scary. She kept calm with an effort. "True. I enjoyed it very much, but I still can't see a future in it. What do you want of me, Alan? A short, mad fling with an older woman? Have you thought what that would do to my reputation? My firm's reputation?"

"Yes, I have, and I can sympathise, but not enough to give up what we could have."

"What we could have can't happen, Alan. Now I'll be brutally honest. I'm scared too."

"Good. At least we agree on something."

They each sipped their wine. Jane felt she needed it. She said, "I've told you, I don't do excess emotion."

It was the wrong thing to say. He seized on it. "So you have. Tell me about this love affair that went so disastrously wrong. There was one wasn't there?"

She didn't know what to say. Alan wouldn't speak and the silence stretched on and on and on.

Eventually she said reluctantly, "Yes, there was a love affair that went disastrously wrong. Yes, it made me the way I am. The person you called an ice woman. Perhaps one day I'll tell you about it, but not yet."

This time Alan broke the silence. "Love affairs usually start slowly," he said. "They start with people getting to know each other, perhaps just as friends. They learn about the other's ideas and prejudices and likes and families and interests and all the things that make a person a person. I'm suggesting we do that. I want to get to know you. Perhaps in time we'll grow together, perhaps we'll grow apart. But we'll have tried."

She thought. "Okay, I'd like to see something of you," she said. "What about sex?"

He shrugged. "I don't want to have sex with you, Jane. I want to make love to you. With you. But only if you do too. The decision would be entirely yours."

She couldn't help remembering the one glorious time they had done so. The decision had been hers then.

"All right," she said. "We'll see something of each other -- as friends. And we'll see how things go."

She drove him back to her office where his car was parked. He rested his hand on her thigh, but the caress was friendly rather than sexual. In the deserted car park she asked him to phone her tomorrow evening, to suggest somewhere where they could meet again.

"Just like a proper love affair," he said lightly, and kissed her goodnight. It wasn't a friendly kiss, it was the kiss of a lover.

"Stop cheating," she said.

Dutifully, sadly, he climbed out of the car. Jane thought she regretted this as much as he did.

Chapter Five

It was both exciting and worrying to hear from Alan the next afternoon. Jane realised she had been waiting impatiently for his call.

"Yesterday we agreed to meet as friends," he said, "and we also agreed that friends get to know each other's background and family and so on. Get to know things that they hadn't considered before. Then they can become lovers."

"*Perhaps* they can become lovers," corrected Jane. "Nothing is certain." But she had to smile. "Alan, you're leading up to something you're not quite sure about. You can't guess how I'll react. Tell me and I promise to think kindly of you."

"Your trouble is that you're too bright," he grumbled. "Why should I tell you anything when you already know what I'm going to say?"

"Rubbish! You have surprised me more than a little in the past few days, more than anyone has in years." Then she felt she had to add, "In more ways than one."

This cheered him up considerably. "I have? Jane, I feel better already."

"So what are you worried about telling me?"

"At first I was wondering if we could meet again this evening, just to be together, but I've since had a phone call from the Rugby Club I'm a member of. You know, the Diehards. I told you I don't play for the first team any more but occasionally I turn out for the second team when I can afford the time. Anyway, this evening the second team is playing a charity match, a friendly in aid of cancer research. Plenty of tickets have been sold and they want to put on a good show. The phone call was to say one of the forwards suddenly had to drop out. There's no one else available, so would I come and play."

Jane didn't have to think twice. "I hope you said yes. I wouldn't have been happy if I learned you had put a few hours with me before helping cancer research."

She could hear the relief in his voice. "That's good to hear, because that's just what I did. So the next step is to ask if you'd like to come to the match. Have a drink afterward in the clubhouse?"

"You don't expect me to join you in one of those communal baths?"

"Sadly, no. Anyway, we've had to have them taken out. Health and safety. I miss them."

"That's a shame. I find the thought of fifteen large muddy men crammed together in one bath and all sharing the soap quite stimulating."

"Miss Gray, at times you shock me. Look, the match starts at half past seven. I'll leave a ticket for you at the gate that says season tickets only, just mention my name. Get there about quarter of an hour before then. Weather report is good, it shouldn't be too cold but wrap up well. There'll be a seat for you in the stand."

"A woman's question, what do I wear for afterwards?"

"Trousers and a sweater. But half-formal, if that makes any sense."

"Got it. I'm looking forward to it."

"Me too. Bye, Jane." He rang off.

Claude was in the office today but she hadn't seen much of him so far. He was busy writing out the plan of a weekend course they intended to run in Russell Manor. She'd shown him her notes on the place and he'd agreed it sounded ideal.

"I'm stepping out tonight," she told him. "I'm going to watch a rugby match and afterward I am invited to a drink in the clubroom."

"The Diehards. You're going with Alan?"

"I am. I'm going to watch him play."

"He'll be playing? I thought he'd largely given it up." Claude nodded, judiciously. "Cunning move on his part. The lad would make a smart manager."

Jane was lost. "He is already a manager, he runs his computer team. What are you talking about, Claude?"

"He wants to impress you. What better way than showing that magnificent body in combat? You'll be bowled over. He's a knight in shining black and purple rugby kit, fighting for the love of his lady."

This thought had not struck her. "Claude, you do go on at times. It's a charity match."

"That makes him even nobler. Incidentally, you'll like the clubhouse. It's like an old-fashioned Gentleman's Club, except they welcome ladies there now. The older members are ... interesting. A good number of the decisions that affect this city are taken in that room. Unofficially, of course, but they are made there."

Then Claude became personal and serious. "I like Alan and you're probably my closest friend. It would please me to see the two of you together. And it would be good for the firm. You have such a lot in common that you'd make a great couple..." His voice trailed away.

"But?"

"You know perfectly well. I'm not going to offer any advice. You're not a fool, you're a very shrewd woman."

"Yes, one who is thirteen years older than my prospective lover."

"So have a fling," says Claude. "Let yourself go a little."

"The thought had come into my head," she admitted. "But then I kicked it out."

*****

Jane had never quite understood the masculine fascination with watching sports. Surely the aim of a sport is to play, not to watch? And how can you think a team belongs to you and your city, when the manager is Portuguese or something and ninety percent of the players have been bought from clubs in other countries?

She took a taxi to the Diehards club. Like her company building, it was in one of the richer suburbs. There were people queuing outside the ground but, as instructed, she walked to the season ticket gate and was greeted by a very courteous, well-educated young man who welcomed her to the club and said he hoped she'd enjoy the match. He told her she should go to the clubhouse when the game had finished, tell the doorman she was Mr Murray's guest, and he would join her as soon as he had showered.

This was all new to Jane. It was like being in a foreign country. She wondered if she should perhaps visit more sporting events. Many of the people she taught were men, it might be useful to have some knowledge of what they were obsessed by.

She found a seat in the stand -- and got a shock. One of the things about being a trainer was that you came into close contact with a group of people for a few days and then often never had reason to see them again. Occasionally they re-appeared in your life, and if they'd enjoyed the course they usually liked to say hello. Now a voice said, "It's Jane Gray, isn't it? How nice to see you. Are you a rugby fan?"

A young woman in a long leather coat had just sat next to her. She went on, "I'm Ann Lloyd. I was on the course you ran at Pittard's six months ago about interview technique. I really enjoyed it and I learned a lot."

Jane remembered her. "You asked about how important eye contact was in an interview. A good question, the group got a lot out of the discussion."

She hadn't answered Ann's first question. It would be foolish to lie. Too often lies came back to confound you. She told a half truth. "I've never been to a rugby match in my life before. One of the home team players invited me. It's Alan Murray. He's going to give some lectures for my firm. We're going to talk about it afterward."

"I know Alan. Ever such a clever man. I'm here to support my boyfriend, Ken Robson, they both play in the same team. Are you going to come here regularly?"

"No. This is purely a business meeting. I don't think I..."

She was interrupted by a mutter of interest from the crowd. Two sets of players trotted out onto the pitch.

"I know nothing about this game," she said to Ann. "It's a bit like football, isn't it?"

It wasn't, as she soon found out. The very idea was heresy. Ann took delight in giving her a clear idea of the rules, and when the game started, kept up a running commentary. That is, when she was not shouting, "Move, Ken, move," or joining in with the home crowd's ritual chant. "Die! Die, Die hard Die."

Jane had to admit to herself she was half inclined to join in. But then she remembered how old she was and that she was a respectable member of the community.

She watched the game, but, of course, she especially watched Alan. It was surprising, she thought, that she could tell traits of his character from the way he played. He was a forward, there was a lot of binding together with others and pushing; a lot of running past the other team's players; a lot of hanging onto the ball and just trying to barge through the opposition. It wasn't random though, whatever it looked like for the first bewildering ten minutes. Jane could see Alan was thinking all the time. He was constantly looking round, assessing the situation, working out where he could run and where he could not.

The ferocity with which he tackled opposing players rather shocked her. It was fair, it was allowed, it was proper, Ann assured her. She had just watched Alan ram his shoulder into the abdomen of one of the opposition and knock him right off the pitch. Was this the man whose hands were so gentle when they had touched, stroked, caressed her naked body? The stray thought made her blush.

Astonishingly, she enjoyed watching the match. At times it was like a chess game. She could see the players positioning themselves where they were likely to be most useful. But it was months since she'd sat and watched someone else do all the work and she was getting restless as the game ended.

"You're going to meet Alan in the club room?" Ann asked. "I'm meeting Ken there. Come on I'll show you the way. It's a nice room, spectators can't get in unless they're members."

Jane had been a bit in doubt about a post-match rugby club meeting. Would there be the singing of vulgar songs, lots of amiable, loud and rude insults and perhaps some horseplay? She remembered the bar at university when the rugby club team had just won an unexpected victory. She only ever went once.

This club room, however, was different. The floor was carpeted a rich Burgundy colour, the walls were wood-panelled, the furniture looked comfortable. No television, but what interested her most was the people there. It was something she'd learned to do, a good trainer assesses the audience quickly. She could read this room, it was full of old money men and younger astute businessmen. She recognised several of them. People were gathered in small groups, having quiet conversations. She had done some of this herself.

Could she do any business here? Then she remembered she was not here to find work, she was here to meet her ... she still didn't know what title to give him. The words "toy-boy" echoed unpleasantly in her head.

"There's Ken," Ann squeaked and a tall man in a blue blazer entered the room, headed for Ann, and kissed her enthusiastically. Ann explained to him that Jane was here to talk to Alan Murray about a job.

"A lot of that happens here," Ken said with a grin. Obviously an observant man.

Then Alan walked into the room and suddenly Jane was a teenager on her first date. He too was wearing what appeared to be the team's dress uniform; blue blazer with crest, white shirt with club tie, pressed grey trousers. His hair was damp, his face reddened after his shower and there was the beginning of a bruise on one of his cheeks. If she felt like a teenager, then there was a touch of the schoolboy about him.

"Hi, Jane, you made it. Good to see you." His smile was so wide that she knew how happy he felt. He moved toward her and quickly she held out her hand for him to shake. No kissing between them in public. He recognised what she was doing and smiled in understanding.

"Did you enjoy the match?" he asked.

"I did, it was a new experience. Watching you rush up and down, scattering the opposition like skittles. I hadn't realised just what a physical man you could be." Of course, she had realised, only too well, but there was no need to go into that now.

Jane indicated Ann, saying they'd met in the stand by chance and that Ann had been on one of her courses. Alan and Ken went over to the bar and Alan bought a round. The conversation was properly general until Ann and Ken left to go out for a meal. Now Jane had Alan to herself.

"Are you glad you came?" he asked. "It's not exactly the evening I had in mind. I thought we might go somewhere a bit more -- well, just you-and-me-ish."

"I like it here. We agreed we need to know a bit more about each other's background. I'm finding out about yours and I like it. It's a different you. You don't usually expect computer geeks to be muscle-bound athletes who jump on top of other men and get covered with mud in the process."

He smiled. "It's more of a collapse than a jump," he pointed out. "Rugby and computing are similar in some ways. Each of them is unforgiving if you make a mistake. I don't like making mistakes."

Now that is an interesting statement, she thought. Before this evening, she'd never imagined playing sport needed too much thought. Perhaps she was wrong.

He took her arm and was about to lead her to a seat in a corner of the room, when a man came over to them. He was late middle-aged, wearing a quite expensive dark suit. He had that air of confidence, of certainty in his own judgement that she recognised in good businessmen. She wondered who he was.

He smiled at Alan. "Congratulations," he said. "You played an excellent game and that last try of yours saved the day. We've not seen you for a while, can't we attract you back to the first team?"

Alan shook his head. "It's tempting, but work must come first. You need to commit yourself fully to play for the Diehards first team."

"True. Work always comes first."

Jane could tell the older man approved of what Alan said. Then he turned to her and said, "Forgive me interrupting, I don't think we've met before?"

"Sorry," Alan said. "I should have introduced you. Sir Arthur, this is Miss Jane Gray. We're talking about doing some work together."

She liked this. Alan knew she didn't want people to suspect there was anything more than work between them. "Jane," he said, "this is Sir Arthur Oswald, the Club President. And many other things besides."

Sir Arthur gave her a courteous smile and they shook hands. "Nice to meet you, Miss Gray."

"It's nice to meet you too, Sir Arthur. Congratulations on pushing through the plans for Beckside Waterfront development and getting the community support and financing. The city will benefit considerably."

She saw his face change slightly, he looked at her more carefully. She was talking his kind of language. "You know of our plans?"

"Only what I've read in the papers, but all my clients think it will bring work to the city, which in turn will be work for them."

He nodded. "Of course, now I remember, I've heard of your firm. Jane Gray Associates. You run industrial training courses. You have a good reputation but we have our own teaching staff, so in general we run in house courses. Have you a card?"

"I'm a business woman," she said with a smile. "I even have a pocket for cards in my bathing costume."

She took one from her handbag and he smiled. "Thank you. This is one I won't be throwing away. If you can just persuade young Alan here to rejoin the first team...?"

"Some nuts are too hard to crack, Sir Arthur," rejoined Jane with a laugh. "Unless they want to break."

"True, true. Well, I suspect it is my turn to buy a round at the bar. I hope we meet again, Miss Gray."

"The feeling is mutual," she said. They shook hands a second time.

Alan took her by the arm and led her to a quiet corner where they could sit. "You never miss a chance do you?" he said cheerfully. "You made an impression there and that's not easy to do."

"I never stop working, you know that."

When they sat a light shone on his face and she looked at the bruise on his cheekbone. It upset her. "Alan, how badly are you hurt? That's a nasty bruise."

He shrugged. "You take things as they come. It doesn't hurt much.

Did you enjoy the game?"

She thought a moment; she wanted to give him an honest answer. "It was interesting -- and impressive. It wasn't like anything in my normal life. Alan, I saw you get tackled late on and you didn't get back up at once. I was worried."

"It's a game. You play it hard or not at all. You ought to understand that, it's just like the way you work."

"I don't risk getting hurt physically."

It was a while before he replied. "Physically isn't the only way of getting hurt. I've seen young computer experts crash and burn through overwork. You can hurt the spirit and the soul just as much as the body."

"I know that only too well."

"If necessary, would you be willing to risk getting hurt?"

"I don't know," she said slowly. "I suspect not."

"I think you might be persuaded to take a risk."

Jane knew they were not talking about rugby now. "It's getting late," she said. "Time to go, I think."

*****

Alan wouldn't hear of her taking a taxi. He had left his car in the players' car park and insisted on driving her back to her office, where her car was waiting.

He drove to the shadiest spot and deliberately switched off the engine and the car lights. Evidently he was not going to drive straight off.

She didn't get out at once. She said, "I've enjoyed this evening and I feel I know you a bit better."

"Good." He put his arm round her neck and kissed her tentatively. She liked it. She liked it a lot so she kissed him back. And then the kissing grew less and less tentative and more and more delightful. Then he said, "I feel like a teenager on his first date. I'm going to try and..."

She felt his hand slide under her sweater. Inside her shirt a finger ran along the top of her bra. She didn't try to stop him, she liked it. His other hand eased her forward in her seat, reached up inside her clothes and undid her bra. Her nipples hardened as he caressed them and she liked this most of all. Well, she could relax for five minutes. She almost felt tempted to let him continue but said, "This is not our first date, but it's going to seem like one. You'd better stop doing that, Alan. It's nice but it'll get us nowhere."

"Don't you like it?"

"I like it a lot. That's why we have to stop. This is the car park of my building. I'm not sixteen any more."

He sighed and took his hands away. She felt unreasonably disappointed but didn't say so.

My Name is Jane Gray

"When can we meet again?" he asked.

"Meet again? All being well -- and my life is full of surprises -- I have all of Saturday off."

"Let's spend it together. You can come to my flat for a meal and see the bachelor squalor I live in," he suggested.

"I'd like that." She knew the last thing his home would be was squalid. "One last kiss then I'm off." She could feel her determination draining away so she slid out of the car. He walked her over to her own, and then waited as she drove away.

Back in her own flat, Jane poured herself a glass of Chablis and stood by the window staring at the dark sea. It helped her think, calmed her.

She was remembering the uncertainties of adolescence. She felt both excited and slightly frightened. She hadn't felt this way since she was fourteen. She wondered what the future might bring. She wondered what she *wanted* it to bring. She didn't know. She was going to spend all Saturday with Alan. Perhaps she'd stay the night. What would be the result?

*****

It was not to be. Next morning there was a phone call from her merchant banker friend Francis Dartington in London. There was no problem with the merger, everything was moving efficiently, but there was some paperwork that had to be gone over and then signed by her in person with a third party looking on as a witness. Francis was very busy, he knew she must be too, but could she come down, perhaps this coming Saturday? It would be a full day's work.

Jane phoned her own brief to check that what Francis had said was right. It was always good to be cautious. She was told it was a legitimate request and that she should go. So she would. She phoned to confirm. She would have to disappoint Alan -- and herself.

So far she hadn't told Alan anything about her agency's merger with the American agency. She hadn't even told her staff, apart from Claude. There was no point announcing it until all was ready. No one would lose out by the change.

The real problem was Alan. She had no idea what to do about him, largely because she had no certainty about her own feelings.

Still, she had always considered sorting out problems was one of her strengths. Come the time, she could cope.

She phoned Alan and told him she had an unexpected business trip to London at the weekend, so their meeting would have to be postponed. He was, as she had expected, very disappointed.

"I'm disappointed too, Alan," she told him, "but we can meet afterward. This is business, it can't be put off." Fortunately, he didn't ask what business. Jane couldn't have lied to him.

"I was looking forward to our day together."

"Think of it this way," she suggested. "We're writing the software of our relationship. We're seeing how things work out."

"My half of the software is already finished and ready to be put into operation."

"Your half? Alan, sometimes you have to work at other people's speed. I'll be in touch."

This time she took the train to London, carrying a briefcase of work with her. She worked on the train and forced herself not to think about their half-planned meal at his flat. As ever, it was easiest when she lost herself in work.

*****

It took most of the day to work through the painstaking details and she was glad when Francis suggested they called a halt. An hour's work next morning when they were fresher should finish things.

All she needed was a relaxing evening in the luxurious hotel where she usually stayed, but she felt out of sorts. She phoned Claude, cheered up a bit at the sound of his friendly voice; told him she was missing Alan and that the day had gone well. She ordered a meal to be served in her room. It was good but she couldn't take much interest in it. She had a bottle of Chablis in an ice bucket but determined not to drink too much of it. Still, that she did enjoy. After her dinner trolley was collected, she had a long bath, and dressed in pyjamas and dressing gown.

Then she phoned Alan.

They'd arranged this, she couldn't phone him earlier because he had decided to put in extra hours at work.

She was surprised at the thrill she got when she heard his voice. "I'm missing you so much, I feel like a schoolgirl," she told him. "I wish you were here."

"So do I. I've just left work, I'm ambling home. What are you going to do now? Go out and see a show?"

"No. I'll stay in my room and work. There's stuff I've brought I can do here. If I can't go out with you, I won't go out at all."

"That is a pity."

"It is. But ... tomorrow will come."

He said, "I have to run. My train's coming in, I'll phone you later tonight. Just before you go to bed."

He was gone, leaving her decidedly unsatisfied. She pulled a chair up to the desk in the room and reached for her briefcase. Work solves everything.

It was about three hours later that he rang.

"Missing me?" he asked.

Jane was resigned now. "What I can't have, I can't have," she told him. "Since I've got to live with it I will. It won't be much longer before we meet."

"Is twenty-four hours not too long?"

"It is too long."

"I have to agree. What about five minutes to wait?"

"Now you're dreaming, just like me."

"I'm not dreaming. I'm in your hotel, phoning from downstairs. I don't think they'll let me into the bar."

She couldn't take this in, what was he talking about? How could he be downstairs? "Why won't they let you into the bar?" she asked, confused.

"I'm not properly dressed. I'm in my work clothes. I was outside the station when I phoned you. I saw there was a train to London in ten minutes so I jumped on it."

"You did what!"

"I got on the train. I wanted to see you tonight. Can I borrow your toothbrush?"

"You're downstairs! Really downstairs! Come up, it's room -- no, on second thought security won't let you. Look, go to reception, I'll phone through and have you escorted up to me. You're downstairs!"

Usually she was cool in emergencies, she could handle most problems. But this! This was something she had never come across before. She looked at herself in the mirror, decided there was just time to brush her hair, no chance of make-up. He'd have to make do with her as she was.

A knock on the door and when she opened it, there was Alan. It was astonishingly good to see him. He was dressed casually, jeans and a tatty black jacket, She wondered what work he had been doing. "This is a surprise," she said.

He grinned. "Do I get a kiss to welcome me?"

"Come inside and we'll see about it." He came inside. Jane moved across to him ... and they kissed ... and kissed ... and kissed.

She slid her hands under his jacket and felt for his bare skin. It was warm but...

"No," he said. "I'm a complete scruff. I've been working, moving heavy stuff around the computer room and haven't had a chance to wash or bath or anything. I was going home but I just jumped on the train."

"I like the smell of you," she said. "But if it bothers you, come and have a shower or a bath."

"Will you get in with me?"

"I've just had one. Daren't have another. Hair, you know."

Alan undressed as Jane ran him a bath and then he slid into it with a sigh. There were bruises on his body which made her wince, but he didn't seem to mind.

She sat on the edge of the bath for a while, smiling at him, washing his back, chatting gently. She fetched him a glass of her wine. Then she became efficient again. He'd said he hadn't eaten much so she sent down for a chicken sandwich and salad. Also two bottles of beer. And would they find a man's toilet set. It all came up fifteen minutes later, by which time he was dressed solely in a large white towel and sitting on the bed.

"You know when you're writing software," she told him, "you sometimes get to a part where it all starts to make sense and you know where you're going and you know you're on the right route?"

"Yes. Done that, been there."

"Well, I'm halfway there. I think that between you and me ... there's something there, Alan. I'm coming round to it."

"You're happy to sleep with me," he said, "and that is wonderful. But now you feel there might be more?"

"Yes ... no ... I've known you so little time. Let's enjoy what there is and see what comes of it."

"Right."

He looked very good dressed just in a towel, but even better out of it.

The sex was different from last time, perhaps because both of them were tired. Their own desires were not the most important thing, both of them were trying hard to please the other.

As they drifted into sleep Jane whispered to him, "I love you." Then, because she was always cautious, she added, "That is, I think I do."

Chapter Six

Next day was -- full would be a good word.

Jane had told Alan about her appointment with Francis at ten o'clock and emphasised that she had to leave the hotel by half past nine.

"Sunday morning is traditionally the time you stay in bed and make love slowly and languorously," he had told her. "Then you sleep a bit longer, wake, and do it again."

"Not this Sunday, Alan. It's the other four-letter word. Work."

"We'll make arrangements." He had leaned out of bed and reached for her alarm clock. "You are used to an early start to the day?"

"Always, if it's necessary."

"I think we both feel that it is necessary. Six o'clock? I'll be out of bed first and make you a cup of tea."

"That sounds fine," she had told him.

And it was fine. They both woke alert, they made love quickly but happily and as she walked out of the hotel with him she felt contented.

"Why are you smiling?" he asked her.

She squeezed the hand that she was holding. "Sometimes, perhaps just for an hour or a day or a week, everything seems to be working out just right. I know it'll change, life is like that, but now is one of those good times."

"An hour, day, or week all seem a bit short. Can't we arrange for a bit longer?"

"We'll make the most of what we have."

Yes, Jane was happy now, but she was on her way to negotiate an arrangement that would involve her moving from England to America. What would happen to them then? *Carpe Diem*, seize the day. Make the most of what they had now. She knew she was avoiding making a decision -- but she couldn't help it.

She took a taxi from outside the hotel and arranged with Alan to meet him at the station in a couple of hour's time. They'd checked the trains, time for a quick lunch before travelling home.

"You'll come to my flat for the bachelor meal I promised you?" he asked.

She shook her head. "Not straight away. I need to go home first, I want to change out of these glad rags and into something more comfortable. And I'll need half an hour on the phone to Claude. This morning's business is important. I'll be over when that's done."

"I want to see as much of you as we can!"

"I feel the same way, but we're both workers, Alan, we know what has to be done, whether we like it or not."

He grinned. "I know what I like best. You like it too."

"Don't be coarse," she said primly -- and then giggled.

*****

The business with Francis was swiftly and completely finished. Perhaps it was the biggest, and final, step toward the complete merger with Walter G. Traekel. Now there could be no going back. It was the right decision she knew, but the firm she had built up over so many years was no longer completely hers. Jane felt her life was moving on.

She blinked as she saw Alan waiting for her by the book shop. He was now dressed in dark cavalry twill trousers, black roll neck sweater, and a brown tweed jacket. In one hand was a neat weekend bag.

"Where's the scruff I parted from this morning?" she asked after he had enthusiastically kissed her.

"I found this vast supermarket. It sold food from a dozen different countries and also had a large clothing section. At first I just selected a pack of socks. Then I got carried away."

"You look very smart."

"I didn't want to let you down. Can't have a smart businesswoman like your good self be seen canoodling with someone who looks a little less than completely hygienic. So bad for your image."

"One; you looked adequately hygienic to me. Two; we are not going to canoodle in public."

He sighed. "I was looking forward to a good canoodle on the train. Just to pass the time you know, it's a boring trip up north."

"I'm going to have to work, as I'm sure you know. How about a quick sandwich and a coffee before we get on the train?"

"As you wish. I'll buy a magazine to read while you're working."

The First Class carriage was almost empty. It was odd sitting opposite him in the train, it seemed interview-like. Alan had wanted them to sit side by side but Jane said too much proximity could be dangerous.

"I don't have a problem with that," said Alan. "By the way, I'd like you to know that I'm wearing those clean new socks."

"That's a relief."

"I'm telling you so that you won't be too alarmed when you feel two socked feet gently stroking your legs."

"Alan! I'm going to work. No canoodling, not even under the table."

"I'm never going to forget you said those words," he grinned. "No canoodling, not even under the table. A warning to stir fright in any man's heart."

"Work!"

The train pulled out of the station. Jane took out her laptop and a sheaf of papers. Alan took the hint as she knew he would. Like her he was a worker. From his pocket he pulled the thick technological magazine that she had seen him buy from the stationers. Soon he was engrossed in it.

After an hour they were offered a drink and she asked for orange juice. Alan had coffee. He continued reading but she closed her eyes and for a moment, reflected on the events of the weekend. What did she think of Alan? As a man that is, not a lover. He was known to have a superbly analytic mind and computer experts are supposed to be emotionless. Yet Alan could be so volatile. He could leap on a train at ten minutes notice with little thought of the consequences. There seemed to be two halves to him. Which half was the stronger? Jane also wondered how she could cope with the two.

There was too much for her to think about at the moment. She opened her eyes, looked down at the last set of figures on her laptop. Some things she could deal with easily. Like figures.

At the end of the journey they parted. She'd already warned him not to kiss her. "This is home territory. I don't want people seeing us and getting the wrong idea."

"Seeing me kissing you might give them exactly the right idea. It's something we both enjoy."

"We can smile and exchange a friendly handshake, just as two business acquaintances would."

"Hooray for friendly business acquaintances. Perhaps our friendly acquaintanceship will develop into something more." He smiled. "You'll come to my flat in a couple of hours?"

"About that."

"Going to bring your pyjamas and toothbrush? I loved the blue silk outfit I saw you in last night."

"Alan! Don't you think of anything but sex?"

"I reckon I think about sex with you as much as you think about it with me. It's wonderful."

There was just enough truth in what he said to keep her quiet.

She took a taxi home and intended to change into something less business-like. Clothes were important in her business, the first impression of someone is often the strongest. So what was suitable for this evening's visit? She decided on something half casual but smart. A sweater and trousers again? Ideal. And, in case he saw it, fresh underwear. A little more dashing than she was wearing earlier.

Next she checked through her notes taken with Francis and on the train. Then she phoned Claude and told him about the meeting.

"It's decided then," he said, "no going back. And you feel just a touch uneasy."

"Just a touch. But, Claude, there's something more I have to think about." She told him about Alan's sudden appearance at her hotel.

Claude whistled. "I like his style. He's turning into one of the world's romantics. You're lucky. Every girl should have a man like that."

"I'm not a girl and I don't want one of the world's romantics. I suspect they cause more trouble than joy."

"You'll never know until you try. Have you told Alan about you moving to America yet?"

The question made her wince. "No. I've even put off thinking about it."

"You're going to have to decide soon, Jane. I like the lad a lot, but a combination of big intellect and gut determination can be dangerous."

"You don't have to tell me, I've already worked it out. I do like being with him."

"That's all important," said Claude.

*****

Jane drove to Alan's bachelor flat. Once, the area had been a village called Henbury, now it was a suburb, swallowed by the enlarging city. There still was a vague sense of community about it.

The flat was in a modern block, surrounded by cared-for gardens and with an area at the back for visitor parking. It would not have been cheap to buy or rent -- proof that Howard Metcalfe was willing to pay very well for a man of Alan's capacities.

The flat was on the top floor. She rang the bell and a voice called through the intercom. "Hiya, Jane. Up to the top floor. There is a lift but I never use it. Exercise is good for you."

"Whatever you can do, I can do too." As she said it, she was glad she wasn't carrying a heavy bag.

He was waiting for her on the top landing. He too had changed, into a t-shirt and jeans and his feet were bare. He was smiling. He whispered, "I've checked, no neighbours watching through their spy-holes, so I can kiss you." He did.

"If you kiss me much more my lips will wear out," said Jane.

He said it would be fun to try and invited her inside. "It's not like your penthouse, but it's home to me."

"I want the tour. I'm going to run my finger along your mantelpiece looking for dust."

"If you find a single smudge then I will sack the butler without a reference. I believe in running a tight ship."

She suspected this last remark was true.

The walls of his living room were painted a calm half-white, half-blue colour. Later, she found out that the whole flat was painted the same. The carpet was a similarly unobtrusive colour, a light grey with no pattern. It too stretched through the whole flat. The furniture was sparse. A couch, a rocking chair, coffee table and a wall of books and shelves, and the television. "A bit minimalist, isn't it?" she suggested.

"People get a flat or a house and promptly fill it with ... stuff. Things you don't need. Things that need cleaning and dusting. I like to keep my life simple."

"I see," she said. "What else can you show me?"

A simple bathroom and an equally functional kitchen with a dining annex. The next door led to a small room with a spare bed in the corner. Here there was apparent confusion. This was where he worked. Three screens over a long desk, two keyboards and a riot of wires, boxes, files, and electronic machines that she didn't recognise.

"This isn't as messy as it looks, is it?" she asked.

There could only be one answer. "No," he said. "I know what and where everything is here. Nothing surplus, nothing not working."

She wished her home could be so organised. She was determined that when she got home she would turn out her underwear drawers and throw some stuff away. "Bedroom?" she asked.

She could feel at home in the bedroom. There were a couple of pictures here, large violent paintings of storms in mountains. A wall of built in units in a light wood and a double bed. The bed had attractive dark blue sheets.

"This bed looks newly made," she said.

He smiled. "I like to keep things tidy. I like to make my bedroom look ... welcoming."

She didn't comment. Saying "it is" could be taken the wrong way.

He looked at his watch. "Six o'clock," he said. "Are you hungry and do you like Thai food?"

It struck her that she had eaten nothing since the snack at the station. "Yes and yes," she answered.

"Good. Since this is my first attempt at entertaining you at home, I decided to spare you the results of my simple bachelor cuisine and ordered a Thai banquet from a place I know down the road. I can recommend it. And I've put a bottle of Chablis in the fridge."

"So what will I get if I am entertained here a second time?"

"I'm a man. I cook a mean curry."

"I can hardly wait."

He glanced out of the window. Long-threatened rain was now spattering the glass. "The easiest thing to do will be for me to jog over and pick it up. No need for you to get wet as well. Will you be happy waiting here?"

"I promise not to open any of your drawers searching for hidden secrets."

"I'm much relieved, but I have no secrets. My life is an open book. I'll be about twenty minutes. See if there's anything you'd like to read in the book case."

He put on socks and shoes, fetched a waterproof jacket from his bedroom, and was gone.

She didn't look for a book to read. Instead she wandered round his flat, from room to room, trying to soak up the atmosphere, trying to decide what kind of man Alan really was. Where people live said so much about them. She guessed he had designed this home himself, that he was contented here. What did it tell her about his character?

After ten minutes she thought she had the answer. This was a calm, ordered, peaceful home. But it did not necessarily belong to a calm, ordered, peaceful man. It belonged to a man who felt the need of self control. The two pictures in his bedroom hinted at this. She suspected there was a passion in Alan, a capacity for sudden, un-thought-out, possibly even foolish action.

Like falling in love with her? And saying so?

She was starting to realise that Alan was not at all like her. He didn't have that complete control over his feelings that she had worked so hard to develop. Or was her control so complete? Having met Alan, having acted so much out of character, she was beginning to wonder.

The intercom by his front door buzzed. Someone downstairs needed to be let in. Jane smiled. He'd been in so much of a hurry to feed her that he'd forgotten his keys.

She pressed the speak button on the intercom. "I hope this is the Thai food delivery service," she said. "Otherwise you're not getting in."

There was a pause. Then a worried female voice asked, "Is this Mr Murray's flat? I'm sorry, have I pressed the wrong bell?"

Oops! Jane had made a big mistake. She tried never to jump to conclusions, too often it left her feeling a fool. Like now. All sorts of people might be calling on him. She wondered who this girl was. The voice sounded quite young.

"This is Mr Murray's flat but he isn't here at the moment," she said. "He should be back in a few minutes."

Another longer pause. "My name's Annette Glover, I'm a friend, I've known Alan for years. Who are you?" Now the voice sounded quite suspicious.

"I'm also a ... friend of Mr Murray, we are working together." Jane could see her Thai meal being delayed, so she tried to be courteous but not welcoming. "Would you ... perhaps ... like to come up and wait to see him?"

"I think I'd better." The chill in Annette's voice matched the chill in hers.

Jane pressed the button to release the front door. "You'd better come up then. He's on the third floor."

"I know. I've been before. Often."

There she was, put in her place.

She was waiting by the open door when Annette Glover arrived. She wouldn't want her to think she wasn't welcome, so she offered her hand and said, "Come inside. It's nice to meet you, Miss Glover. My name's Jane Gray."

Her hand was squeezed briefly and dropped. Then they surveyed each other.

Jane didn't know what Miss Annette Glover saw, but whatever it was, it didn't fill her with joy. A little too late she realised that, although she thought she had dressed casually, she had also dressed expensively. Her shoes were good, her trousers were from the best ladies outfitter's in town, her sweater the lightest of angoras.

She could tell by Annette's stance that the girl had decided not to be brow-beaten. She was hostile. Her shoulders were hunched, her face resolutely non-smiling, she avoided eye-contact. She was wearing a long, rain-speckled anorak and shook herself so that drops fell onto the carpeted floor. Age, mid twenties. Face, quite pretty.

They walked down the little hall. Annette took off her anorak and without saying anything went into the bathroom to hang it up. A clear demonstration of the territorial imperative; she had been here before, knew her way around, expected to be welcomed.

Interesting, Jane thought. Perhaps a bit upsetting.

Back in the living room, Annette sat on the couch. She was wearing jeans, a roll-necked sweater in an unsuitable red colour. "Where has Alan gone?" she asked. "Will he be long? I've not seen him for a week or two. I've dropped in to invite him round for tea."

She was not going to like what Jane was about to tell her. Oh well, let battle commence. "That'll be a bit difficult," Jane said. "He's gone round to the Thai restaurant for a takeaway. He's invited me here for dinner."

"Dinner? He's invited you here?" This was clearly not the best news Annette had ever heard. "Why should he invite you for dinner?"

Jane decided to try to calm things a little. "I approached him to give a series of lectures for me. We have the programme to discuss. He thought that this would be a good way of doing it."

"You want him to give lectures?"

"I run an agency that supplies courses to various businesses. I employ a number of specialist lecturers. Alan is -- or will be -- one of them."

If she thought this might placate Annette she was wrong. "Why pick on Alan? He's got a good job already."

"I know. I offered him some part-time work because I was impressed by him." Jane decided it was time that she got a few answers herself. "You say you've known Alan long?"

"All my life. We grew up in the same street, our mothers are old friends. We were always in and out of each other's houses."

Annette now seemed a little calmer, a little more confident. She felt she'd established some kind of tenant's rights. Jane thought she'd ask the big question. First she stared at Annette's left hand. No ring. "You're not engaged or anything like that?"

Annette flinched at this, obviously it was not fair to be so direct. She looked at Jane malevolently and said, "No. Not really. I've not seen so much of him recently, he has been very busy. There's a sort of understanding between us. He knows he can rely on me for anything."

This made Jane feel slightly sorry for the girl.

The flat door banged open. Alan's voice shouted, "Hi, sweetheart. I'm so hungry I could eat a horse -- but they had no horse left so I picked beef and chicken instead. I hope you..."

Then he walked into the living room, saw Annette, and his face registered shock and horror in equal amounts. "Annette! What are you doing here?"

If he needed to ask that question he must be dimmer than Jane had thought.

Annette certainly knew what she was doing. She leapt to her feet, ran across the room, threw her arms round him, and kissed him. This was hard for Alan as he had a brown carrier bag with oriental writing on the side in each hand. All he could do was stand there and wait. Jane registered that the contents of the bags smelled wonderful. She realised she was hungry.

Eventually the longish kiss ended and Alan was released. Annette obviously thought that she was ahead of the game and rapidly said, "I've not seen you for so long and I came round to invite you for tea."

Alan was recovering. He looked at Jane as Annette was nuzzling his left ear and grimaced, indicating that this occurrence was most unfortunate. Jane almost felt sorry for him.

Firmly, he pushed Annette away from him. "Annette, it's nice to see you but it's not a good time. Miss Gray here has offered me some very well paid work and she's here for us to talk it over. It'll take quite a long time so I offered her dinner. I'm afraid you'll have to go and leave us to work."

"But I haven't seen you for weeks! When I phone, you always say you're busy working. This is me, Annette, remember?"

"I remember. I am always working. Like tonight."

"Well, work then! I won't disturb you, I'll sit here quietly or in your bedroom with a book like I used to and when ... Miss Gray leaves we can have some time together."

For a moment Jane remembered Alan hitting the big man in Harvey's Mill. She realised then, he could be patient for a while but there was that tough streak in him, not too far below the surface, which would eventually come out. Like now.

"Annette! When you used to stay *quietly reading* while I worked -- you interfered every five minutes. You drove me away. I spent more time in the library than I did at home. So, you are not going to sit here and read. You're going home."

"You just want to be alone with this woman and..."

"Stop before you say something you'll be very sorry for."

What a voice! It was quieter than before but it held such ... menace, was it? Jane shivered.

"All right," mumbled Annette. "My coat's in the bathroom."

Alan escorted her out of the room. Jane didn't shout a cheery "Goodnight, Annette," after her. In the hallway, Annette said loudly, "When can I come round, then? Don't use work as an excuse."

"I'll ring."

Jane heard the flat door bang shut. Alan returned, his face apologetic. Jane put a finger to her lips. "Don't say a word about anything. Those two bags smell so good and I'm so hungry that -- did I hear you mention a horse?"

A small smile indicated that he knew what she was doing. "It will take exactly five minutes for me to serve the meal I have prepared."

"Prepared as in purchased?"

"A repast by any other name would smell as savoury. Come and sit down, we can chat while I lay the table."

She was impressed by the way he'd picked up what she wanted. He knew there must be some discussion of Annette, but food came first.

It was superb. Thai cooking at its not-too-over-spiced best. The chilled wine was the perfect accompaniment. As dessert they had a spoonful of very expensive fruit and spirit ice cream and ginger biscuits.

"A bachelor's cunning way of suggesting he is sophisticated," he explained. "I've loved ice cream since I was spilling it down my bib. There's always a supply in my freezer. Sometimes, like if I'm working through until two in the morning and nothing is going right. I sneak myself a bowlful and the world seems a better place. When I am giving these talks for you, I'm going to mention that if you have a problem at work, then coffee is a valuable but dangerous aid. Ice cream on the other hand is not dangerous but works as a stimulant just as well."

"Even if it makes you fat?" But for some weird reason, the thought of him having a stimulating ice cream in the small hours of the morning made him more loveable. Jane was not sure why.

When the meal was finally -- and sadly -- over, he suggested she go to sit in the living room while he cleared away. "Don't offer to help," he said, "this room is too small and you don't know where anything goes. I'll be through with coffee in a few minutes."

It made sense. She planned what she needed to say next. For a start, she deliberately sat on the couch. She didn't want the distance between them that her sitting in the rocking chair would bring. She knew that there would be no danger of Alan sitting in it. He'd want to be by her side, nearly touching.

She wanted him to.

He came in, bringing a tray of coffee and for a moment or two they sat there comfortably, silently. The coffee, as she might have guessed, was excellent.

Then, painfully, he began, "Jane, about Annette, there's something you..."

She leaned over and kissed him gently on the cheek. "We're going to talk about her," she said. "I need to and I think you want to. I can guess a lot of the story, and it doesn't matter. How would it be if I asked the questions and you answered them as best you can?"

"That suits me fine."

"She told me you grew up together, that your mothers were, and are still, neighbours and friends."

"True. We saw an awful lot of each other." For a moment a smile showed on his face. "She was the first girl I ever slept with. Mind you, I was six and she was three. A sleepover one night."

"I can forgive you. So you were friends. What happened as you got older?"

He shrugged. "We walked to school together, saw a lot of each other, but we had other friends. I went to university three years before she left home. She's an infant teacher now. I graduated, then a PhD at Cambridge, then a spell in America, and now I'm working for Howard. We vaguely kept in touch, I'd take her out for old times' sake when I was home. Now she's only fifteen minutes walk away and thinks things should be as they were. She hasn't moved on."

"She thinks things should be as they were?"

Now Alan did look uncomfortable. "Well, for a while, just after I'd taken my first degree, when I was living back here at home, one summer we got ... quite close."

"You slept with her. Her first time?"

A faint blush on his cheek and it was a while before he replied. "Yes. Mine too." When Jane didn't comment he went on, "It petered out when I had to go back to Cambridge and there was little chance of us seeing each other. Besides it had just been a ... a..."

Jane felt for Annette. Her voice was cold as she said, "A holiday romance? A way of spending time, not being bored, while you were at home? When you said the affair petered out, who did the petering?"

It was quite a while before he answered. "I did. You're quite right in what you're hinting. I did tell her, but she wouldn't accept it. She cooed that of course, I had my career to think of, but she was happy to wait. So when I moved back here, it was all too obvious to her that we were meant for each other and my job with Harold was her reward. Nothing I can say will persuade her otherwise."

"Do you see anything of her now? Socially, I mean."

"We've had the odd meal. I've been invited to her mother's house with my mother. It's always uncomfortable for me because the three of them insist on behaving as if Annette and I are a couple. We're really not."

"Right. I've got the picture." Part of Jane was sorry for Alan, part of her was exasperated at a man who could let himself be trapped in this way.

He asked ruefully, "Where does this leave us? Has meeting Annette made any difference?"

Jane rubbed her eyes. "I had a hard day yesterday. Your coming to London was a surprise, but a lovely one. Today hasn't been easy and this evening certainly wasn't the way I'd anticipated having a meal with you. The result is that I'm tired and I want to go to bed."

"You want to go home. Fair enough. I can understand that."

"No," she said, irritated. "I want to stay here. I want to go to bed with you. I just don't want to do any more talking."

*****

Alan was in the bathroom. Jane had showered and cleaned her teeth. She lay in his beautiful blue-sheeted bed and she wondered. She thought he was sincere in what he'd said about Annette. But the girl was his contemporary, whereas Jane was thirteen years older. What sort of future could they have?

Chapter Seven

It felt good to get back to work next day. Jane could put Alan to the back of her mind for a while. She had a quick half hour with Claude, going over new problems thrown up by the future merger.

She admitted she'd spent the night with Alan. "Have you told him you'll be going to live in America soon?" he asked at once.

"No," she said, feeling wretched. "I'm still having difficulties coming to terms with our relationship and rationalising what I want and what he thinks he wants."

"He sounds like a passionate man. Remember, sudden romantic actions -- like coming down to London on a whim -- are fine until they go wrong, which they have a habit of doing."

This made her think.

She worked. There were invoices to chase up, suggestions for new work, and putting together a brochure for weekend courses at Russell Manor. She also drew up possible plans for a couple of full week courses.

She was enjoying the work, it was calming her down. Then she realised, once again, she was using work as a displacement activity instead of working out what to do about Alan.

Just at that moment she had a call from her switchboard. "Will you accept a phone call from a Mrs Murray, Jane? She won't say what it's about." The receptionist sounded affronted. "She says it is personal, but she's sure you'll want to take the call."

Mrs Murray? For a ghastly moment she thought it might be Alan's wife that he hadn't got round to mentioning. *Idiot*, she told herself. Hadn't he mentioned only yesterday that his mother lived nearby? She thought for a second and then flicked the switch that automatically recorded the call. She wasn't taking any chances where Alan was concerned. "Thank you," she said. "Put her on."

The voice she heard was clear and commanding. "Good morning, Miss Gray. My name is Ursula Murray. I believe you know my son Alan."

She could keep calm. She did. "Certainly I know him. I've approached him on a professional matter. Why are you asking? I'm sure you understand I can't talk about business."

"I do understand. But a professional matter is not the whole story, is it? I'm more interested in the personal. I'd like to meet you, Miss Gray. It's in both our interests. Have you any time this afternoon?"

Jane was astonished. Alan wasn't a child. Since when did a twenty-eight-year-old's mother start interfering in her son's relationships? "I'm sorry, I'm very busy. Why do you want to meet me?"

This woman, like Jane herself, didn't like being taken for a fool. Her irritation showed in her voice. "Obviously, to talk about my son," she snapped.

"I wouldn't dream of meeting to talk about Alan unless he was present. I have to tell you I intend to phone him to tell him about this call."

"In your situation I'd do the same. You might not believe it, but I have my son's best interests at heart -- and to a certain extent, yours. I want to keep this affair as quiet as possible. If you won't meet me, I'll consult my cousin. Ask what he thinks about the matter."

"Your cousin?" Jane asked.

"My cousin, Howard Metcalfe. Didn't Alan tell you that we're related?"

"No, he didn't. Is this a threat, Mrs Murray?"

"Mentioning family relationships is not a threat. All I'm asking for is a few minutes of your time."

"I don't like blackmail," said Jane crisply. "But I'm willing to talk to you for ten minutes at two thirty this afternoon in my office."

"Until then, Miss Gray." Ursula Murray rang off.

Jane drummed her fingers on the desk. Then she asked Claude to come to her office and played the call to him.

He considered for a moment or two. Then, "First, Howard Metcalfe knows much of his firm's recent success is due to us. He admits this. He might be angry with you, but the businessman in him won't let him do anything stupid. He'll keep us on. Second, my reading of Alan. If any of this comes out, he'll leave Everett's. Howard will not be happy about that. There is a huge demand for IT experts. Alan would have no trouble finding an equally good job." He grinned mischievously. "Perhaps even with us."

Jane flinched. "Don't say that! It would be madness for all sorts of reasons."

She phoned Alan on his mobile, but there was no answer. She tried his work number but he was not there either. One of his team told her he'd been summoned to another branch of the firm to troubleshoot a problem. "He'll have switched off his mobile because he always does. Try later. "

*****

A corner of Jane's office was arranged informally; easy chairs facing each other over a coffee table. Jane arranged for coffee to be served and asked Claude to be accidentally in the foyer to meet and bring Mrs Murray to her. She'd want his opinion of her later. Then she waited for two thirty.

She was sitting behind her desk when there was a tap at the door and Claude ushered a lady in. "Mrs Murray, your visitor," he said.

"Mrs Murray? I'm Jane Gray," She stood, walked round her desk and shook hands, firmly. "Would you like to sit down?" She gestured towards the seating area.

"You're not going to have me sit opposite you at your desk? Like an errant student and her teacher?"

Apparently Mrs Murray was ready to fight. Jane was not. Not yet.

"Why would I?" she said, "May I take your coat?"

As she hung it up, she noticed the label. This coat was expensive. "Coffee or tea?" she asked. When coffee was requested she asked Claude to see to it and he left, as had been planned.

Mrs Murray and Jane sat opposite each other. Jane noticed the way her visitor was looking round, assessing the office just as she would have done herself. She suspected Alan's mother was a bit like her. Not someone to be dealt with easily. She was dressed in a smart blue suit, had a matching silk scarf. Her hair had recently been well styled, her jewellery was expensive but not obtrusive. She was perhaps ten years older than Jane. Not something to be dwelled on at the moment.

"You have a look of your son," said Jane. "The same jaw line, same high cheek bones."

"True. People say we are alike in character, too. I won't tell you how."

Jane took a flyer. "You're usually calm, thoughtful, and reserved," she said, "but if pushed too hard you are capable of sudden possibly excessive outbursts of anger -- or affection. Is that it?"

A look of reluctant respect crept into Ursula's eyes. "You are very clever, Miss Gray. Fortunately for this discussion, I have learned to control my temper. Alan has improved since he was a child."

"I am a busy woman. May we get to the discussion?"

A small smile indicated a point was about to be made. "I'm the Principal of Long Marton College of FE. I get to hear about every educational institution in this city. Jane Gray Associates has a very good reputation as far as business training courses go."

For a moment Jane was irritated with Alan. All right, he was technical, not in business, but he should have warned her who his mother was. Long Marton College, with the advantage of paid staff and permanent buildings, had undercut her on several occasions and grabbed some of the work that should have been hers. "As do you," she said smoothly. "Are you here to propose a merger?"

Ursula Murray cut abruptly to the chase. "Last night you went to dinner at my son's flat. There was an unexpected extra guest, Annette Glover, who was not made welcome. After dinner you stayed the night -- at least your car was still outside at half past midnight. This leads me to the conclusion that you have a sexual relationship with Alan."

Jane didn't protest or show that she was shocked. She recognised an adversary when she came up against one. She knew she had to play it cool, so she smiled dismissively. "It is possible for two people to share a two-bedroom flat and not have sex," she suggested. "I was over the limit for driving, so Alan..."

Mrs Murray shook her head. "I've known Annette for many years, she is more astute than you realise. From her description of the behaviour of you and Alan, I am certain -- as she was -- that the two of you were lovers. She caught him looking at you the way he used to look at her."

This shocked Jane a little. "He used to look at Annette that way? Annette was the one who saw my car still outside at half past twelve?"

"She was. She couldn't sleep."

"I feel sorry for her. It was obvious that she is hopelessly in love with Alan. I believe he has outgrown her."

"And grown into you?"

Now that was nasty. "I don't care to discuss my relationship with your son with you, Mrs Murray, but..."

A knock at the door. "Come in," called Jane.

Jane offered a regular place to a small local catering college and every three months a young intern came in to learn something about the practicalities from her kitchen. Seventeen-year-old Kylie was a willing but nervous young girl and this was the first time she had served in the office. "Just put the tray here on the table, Kylie," said Jane, "and we'll pour it. Did you percolate the coffee and arrange the tray yourself?"

"Yes, Miss."

"Enjoying your first week here?"

"Yes, Miss. Cook is ever so good to me."

"I'm pleased to hear it. Off you go then." Kylie left.

Mrs Murray was looking at her sardonically. "I could hear myself talking then," she said. "You'd make a good teacher."

Jane was not having that. "I already am one," she said. "I was telling you that I don't care to discuss my relationship with your son without him being present. May I also say that I'm going to be gracious and for the moment forget your attempt to blackmail me by telling tales to Howard Metcalfe. You're Alan's mother. What do you think he'd do if I told him what you'd said?"

"I'd have to take my chance." It was said warily.

"Let's have some coffee," she said. "Calm down a little."

She poured out two cups. They sipped and smiled at each other.

"Excellent coffee," said Mrs Murray.

"Have a piece of shortbread," Jane replied, and pushed the plate forward.

There were times when she had run courses for both management and work-force on negotiation skills. She had acted as a facilitator, trying to reconcile two apparently fixed positions. It was fascinating work and on a number of occasions she had managed to indicate where there might be a middle path to satisfy two apparently opposed sides. She might as well try out her skills.

"What do you have against me?" she asked.

"Simple. You're too old for Alan. Having children would be difficult if not impossible. Bringing them up would be a nightmare. You'd be old and decrepit while he was still young. Neither of you would be happy."

"There are many documented cases of happy marriages between people who have a large age gap," Jane suggested.

"And plenty of undocumented cases of unhappy marriages."

Jane had to concede this point.

"Do you love him?" Mrs Murray asked bluntly.

"Yes," she said after a while. "I think I do. Or I could. He thinks he loves me."

"He *thinks* that he loves you?"

Jane knew she'd pick up on that. "He's still young. Remember what it was like?"

"I've been widowed for twenty years, but yes."

"No occasional flings?"

She flushed. "I'm not here to answer questions about my private life, Miss Gray."

"No, you're here to try to interfere with mine." Jane remembered she was trying to mediate. "Look," she said, "believe it or not I sympathise with you. I agree entirely that a marriage with a thirteen year age gap would be difficult. Alan may well come to realise this." She had to pick her next words with care. "Let me offer you this: we'll forget this meeting ever happened. I have a genuine regard for your son. The last thing I want to do is to hurt him. I intend to go on seeing him. Perhaps we'll have a fling. But I promise you that in no way will I let it progress to anything more than that for say a year. By then everyone will know their own mind."

"Am I to believe that?"

"If you know anything about my firm you will know that we have a reputation for honesty. That comes from me."

Another silence. Then Mrs Murray stood and said, "I suppose I'll have to agree to that, and I must admit it's more than I hoped for. So thank you. I do believe that you have a genuine regard for my son, but, you know, Miss Gray, I don't much like you. You remind me too much of myself."

"I'll take that as a compliment."

*****

After Jane had seen Mrs Murray out, she poured herself another coffee and considered her promise to Alan's mother. She would not give Alan up. She had a genuine regard for him, yes, but she felt more than that ... she felt she loved him.

The hard, analytical part of her brain told her this could be the passing fancy of a woman who had been working too hard and was having difficulty with her hormones. In her business career she had seen disastrous decisions made by otherwise astute business-women of a certain age. She didn't think this was her but she had to accept it was a possibility. If they agreed their relationship was essentially casual and loving for a year -- well, it would give her a breathing space. It would give them both the chance to find out if being together would last.

Sometimes it happened this way. The minute she decided what she would say to Alan, her phone rang. Her personal phone, not the switchboard.

"My mate said a posh bird phoned me earlier," a voice said. "You're the only posh bird I know. Incidentally, this is not going through the firm's switchboard."

"I confess, it was me who phoned. Your mobile was switched off. Congratulations on learning about switchboards. I gather you're working late tonight. Until when?"

"I should be setting off for home about half past nine."

"Whose home?"

There was silence for a minute. Then, "Does that mean what I think it means?"

"Yes. I'll have some supper ready for you. There's something I need to say to you, and the quicker the better."

She could hear the doubt in his voice. "Not again, Jane. Is this going to be good news or bad?"

"Don't worry, I think you'll consider it good news. See you about ten." She rang off.

Then Claude tapped and entered. "I saw Mrs Murray leaving," he said. "She looked neither triumphant nor upset."

"We've come to an agreement," said Jane, and told him what it was.

He nodded. "A real mediator's agreement. Good if all the parties to it agree."

"I'm seeing Alan tonight. I'll tell him it's what I think is best."

"He's got you for a year and no trouble from anyone. The lad's got it made."

"So have I," she said. "Or so I think."

*****

Alan seemed to be learning about discretion. He phoned Jane from his car saying he'd be arriving in ten minutes. She told him there was a spare parking place in the garage, she'd come down to open the doors.

She was waiting when his car swung into the drive, used her fob to open the gates, and waved him straight inside. Then she closed the gates and went in to meet him.

He smiled at her and looked around. "We're alone," he said. "This is not a kissing-free zone."

He took her head between his hands and gently kissed her. She relaxed into the embrace. In his arms she'd be happy to stand there for ... But then she looked up at him. Close up, she could see he looked tired, there were lines round his eyes and he had the shadow of a beard. "You must be exhausted," she said. "You didn't get enough sleep last night." Then she blushed as she remembered why.

"Or the night before," he returned with a grin. "Tired or not, I think the past two nights have been the best of my life. Are we going to turn that into the best three nights?"

"Upstairs with you. I've got supper waiting and I've bought you a couple of bottles of good beer. Then we have to talk seriously."

"I don't like the serious talk. But supper and beer sounds good. Do we have to stop holding and kissing?"

"For the moment, yes." Jane smiled. It was good to be with him.

They took the lift up to her flat. She opened one of the beers and suggested he had a bath, there was a dressing gown he could borrow afterward. Then she put out supper on a tray. Nothing exciting: rolls, salad, and a variety of meats and cheese. The beer on one side and she had a glass of wine.

Having a bath didn't take him long. Was he in a hurry? He came in, dressed somewhat inadequately in a silk dressing gown and smelling of her expensive bath oil. Supper was served on the coffee table.

"Eat and drink first," she told him, "then we'll talk. How tired do you feel?"

He shrugged. "I could have done without the call to the other branch. A lot of stuff had built up, I had to clear the decks. I'm on top of it now. I could even take a few days off if I wanted. I've got holiday time banked."

"I can tell you don't work for yourself."

"So what are we to talk about seriously? I'm tired and I could do with going to bed." Then he grinned and added, "I'm not that tired."

No way was he going to be the only one allowed to make suggestive remarks. "Neither am I," she said. "As, if you're lucky, you'll find out. Eat your nice supper."

He obviously had not had much time for meals that day. He ate most of what was on the table. It gave Jane an odd pleasure. Then she cleared away the dishes, left them stacked for the moment, and poured herself another glass of wine.

"Talk time," she said. "I've been thinking about this a lot, about what you are to me and what our future is. And before we go any further, because I can see you're about to object, I want to say you mean an awful lot to me and I do hope we have a future -- of some kind."

"Good so far," he said cautiously, "except for the phrase *of some kind*."

"We are starting -- have started -- a love affair. It makes me very happy but also apprehensive because of what I know people will think and say. That has to be important to both of us, career-wise I'm thirteen years older than you!"

"I know. And I don't care. I also don't care too much about what other people might think."

"So speaks the young man," she said feelingly. "That's exactly what I mean. I've got more to lose than you, but that doesn't mean I don't want to try. What I don't want is to do it in the full glare of the public eye. Alan, what I'm suggesting is that we give ourselves a year. After that, we think again. There's to be no commitment on either side, no talk of a long-term or even permanent relationship. We see each other; if we want to, we sleep together, but we don't make a big production out of it. We don't have to see or hear from each other every night. Sometimes we're seen out together and people will talk, but no kissing in public. We don't buy a house together or move into the other's flat. Both of us have the right to end the relationship at any time without recrimination. A completely happy but casual year, Alan. A year long fling, if you like. It could be good."

To Jane's dismay, he didn't look thrilled. "I'm twenty-eight. That's a bit old for a fling."

"I'm thirteen years older than you and I'm willing to risk it. Okay, it's your turn to talk."

He didn't answer at once. Instead he frowned. Jane could almost see the thoughts passing through his head, each considered, accepted or rejected, then filed. A true IT brain. Eventually he sighed. "I can see a lot of sense in what you say. For me there's a lot of good in it. I get to see you as much as is possible, which will be wonderful because I'm now finding you central to my life, but you are making it clear you don't own me. I feel there ought to be a catch. I agree, Jane, but there are two things I must ask."

"Which are?"

"One, never again, unless it's really necessary, mention your age as if it was important. It isn't. Two, can we go to bed now?"

"I thought you'd never ask." She reached over and took his hand. "The bedroom is this way."

She had only known him a few days. There had been a fair amount of kissing, but she could count them, this was only the fourth time they had really made love. It was getting -- not better, that would be impossible -- but less experimental, less clumsy, if that was the word. Their bodies seemed to know each other, to recognise, to anticipate what was needed, what would give pleasure. There was more talking than before. Their previous love making had been almost silent, apart from those glorious culminating sighs and moans when their passion reached its final ecstatic goal. Now they could whisper to each other. Or call out. It was magic

Then there was that sense of release, of satisfaction, of completion. The night wasn't yet over. One last kiss and they drifted into sleep. Jane knew that when she woke in the night there'd be someone beside her, a warm body, offering comfort and a sense of belonging. She could listen to his deep breathing, feel the gentle rise and fall of his chest. She was not alone. It felt good.

*****

They might have been devoted to each other, but there was something else they were equally devoted to. Work. Jane woke Alan quite early; they washed, dressed, and breakfasted quickly and were both out of the building by half past seven next morning. This was late for her but she was happy. She suggested they meet in two days time for an evening drink at his rugby club. Afterward he could come back and spend the night at her flat.

"You just want to meet Sir Arthur Oswald again," he teased. "You're using me for my important connections."

Primly, she said, "The thought never crossed my mind. Although, if he is there..."

He laughed and kissed her. "I'll get you a contract. I'll tell him I'll rejoin the first team if he employs you. I'll risk health and strength, offer my body so you can get work."

"I'm quite capable of getting my own contracts, thank you. For various reasons I need your body in perfect condition myself. Off you go or you'll be late!"

She felt happy as she drove to work.

*****

There were always problems at work -- perhaps that's why she liked it so much. Big problems, small problems, intermediate sized problems. There was one on her screen when she sat down to her first cup of coffee. It was intermediate size, shading up to big.

For the past five years she had been extending her work into Europe. She had subsidiary agencies in France, Germany, Spain, and Switzerland. This was one reason why Walter G. Traekel was so eager to take her over. It was a foothold in Europe.

Now, in front of her was an e-mail from one of her lecturers in France. Giselle Leblanc worked almost full time for her in a college near

Tours. The message held both challenge and an opportunity. First, Giselle had been asked -- unexpectedly -- if she could double the size of two of her classes. She could, she wanted to, she would be paid more. The problem was that as well as Jane's permission, this course needed a set of discs and a complete workbook for each student and it was in ten days time! Jane had the workbooks printed locally -- she would have to have a fresh set printed and dispatched to Tours express. It could be done. Just. The challenge in the e-mail was that the college also wanted to expand an entire branch of its management department. They would need new staff. They wanted to talk to her -- urgently and in person -- as soon as possible.

She thought for a moment and then buzzed Claude.

He looked at the message, pursed his lips, and said, "This is a big opportunity for the firm, of course you've got to go. I'll get the workbook order started. You can kill two birds with one stone. Take your car over to Tours, carrying the workbooks and stay to talk to the college. Have a bit of a holiday."

"What about my work here?"

He grinned. "I'm already taking stuff over that you used to do, for when you leave for America. I can cope."

Jane loved driving and she loved France and she hadn't been for eighteen months. "I'll do it," she said.

"Book now before you change your mind."

She always used the same travel agency, they treated her well -- as they should, the amount of work she gave them. She was put through to Lisa, the girl she usually dealt with, told her what she wanted and Lisa promised to ring her back in an hour.

Then she realised something and the realisation shocked her a little. She wouldn't see Alan for over a week. She would miss him.

An hour later Lisa phoned and told her she was booked on the overnight ferry from Portsmouth to San Malo. She had reserved an outside cabin, Jane liked to look out of the porthole at night. From San Malo it was a long but easy drive to Tours. She was booked back on the ferry the following Saturday afternoon. It might be a good idea to drive to San Malo on the Friday and spend the night there before catching the day ferry back. Should Lisa book a hotel? Jane decided yes.

Now she was looking forward to her trip. But she would still miss Alan.

*****

For Wednesday they had arranged a late meeting at the Rugby Club. The idea was to have a couple of drinks and a chat and then come back to her flat where he would again stay the night.

She was looking forward to it, but took her laptop as camouflage.

They could look at it together. Two colleagues having a friendly drink and working at the same time. For a change she dressed in a blouse and skirt and allowed herself a pair of heels. They weren't suitable when she'd gone to see the match. She took a taxi to the club, she would travel back home in his car.

The taxi dropped her outside the club doors and a minute later she saw Alan loping toward her. He must have been watching for her out of the window. She liked that.

It was interesting inside the clubroom. She recognised several of the faces from the previous week, but the people she didn't recognise all had the same air to them. This was a place where business was done. "I could join this club," she said to Alan, "It's full of the kind of people I work with."

"A lot of business is done here. Surprisingly, we also get occasional courses being run here, there's a small suite of rooms upstairs. I'll show you them later. But there's a price for being a member. You have to watch a certain number of matches per season and be prepared to shout 'die die die' quite loudly."

"I think I've changed my mind, even though I did like watching you play."

He squeezed her hand.

They sat at a small table and he had a beer and she had glass of white wine. They chatted about nothing much in particular, she told him about her planned trip to France and he said he'd miss her, as she would miss him. Occasionally people drifted over and said hello but mostly they were left on their own, especially when she took out her laptop and they studied it.

She was on her second drink when a group of men came down from upstairs. She noticed that Sir Arthur was one of them.

"Committee meeting must be over," said Alan. "Now I can show you the rooms you might want to use. Leave your laptop here, it'll be quite safe."

Jane hesitated. "My life is in that laptop. Would you leave anything like that of yours lying around?"

"No," he said after a moment's reflection, so she picked it up. She wouldn't let him carry it. As she said, it was her life.

The upstairs rooms would be very useful for a small course and she made a note to write to the secretary and ask for a list of charges. Then she and Alan went back to finish their drinks.

"Then we can go home," he said with a beaming smile. "Your home, that is."

Things always happen when you least expected them.

They were walking down the stairs back to the bar, when the laptop started to slip from under Jane's arm. She grabbed for it and missed her step. Before she realised what was happening she had tripped and was half running, half staggering, down the steps.

On the bottom step she missed her footing completely. Her right foot twisted and all her weight descended on it. She felt something crack in her ankle and fell face forward. The pain in her ankle was agonising. She had kept hold of her laptop.

"Jane, are you all right?" came Alan's concerned voice and she somehow rolled over to look at him kneeling by her side.

"Been better," she said.

*****

If you had to have a serious leg injury there were worse places to have it than in a rugby club. They were used to that sort of thing. Her fall had been heard; among the crowd of concerned onlookers who rushed in was a doctor. He took charge.

"Alan, move back a bit, give me some room. You lot get back in the bar, you're in the way. I'll see to the young lady."

She liked the young lady description.

"My name is David Kershaw, I'm a doctor. I don't want you to move for a couple of minutes, while I do a quick check-up. Your name is..."

"Her name's Jane Gray," came Alan's taut voice. "She's a friend of mine."

"Right, Jane. Now breathe steadily, don't worry about anything. Close your eyes if you like. Tell me where the pain is."

She felt his hand take her wrist, knew he was checking her pulse. "My right ankle hurts like fury," she managed to gasp. "Otherwise no great damage."

"Good. Head and neck all right?" Now she felt his hands lifting her head, fingers gently probing.

"No problem at all."

"Alan, did you see her hit her head as she fell?"

"I watched her fall. She was upright, staggering but just keeping her balance until she hit the bottom step and turned her ankle. Then she fell. Her head was never at risk." Alan's voice was neutral, all emotion wiped away. She knew that this was his way of keeping control.

"Right. Pick her up, Alan, and carry her into the changing room and lay her on the table there."

"I don't need to be carried. If you can help me up I'll walk..."

"My rugby players are more disciplined than you," came David's amiable voice. "You're temporarily in my care, so do as you're told."

So she did. The club had a very good first aid kit, David sent Alan to fetch it. She was brought a mug of tea with much sugar in it and told it was good for her. It might have been good, but sugar...? With the tea came two white tablets. "Pain killers." David explained.

She had felt shaken but now she was recovering and starting to feel embarrassed. Falling downstairs? She felt a fool!

Whatever the pain killers were, they were effective. The agony in her ankle was starting to lessen.

"There's no nurse here," David said. "So I'll take off your shoes and then Alan and I will turn our backs and you can wriggle out of your tights. I need to have a close look at that ankle."

"When I came out to meet you this evening," she said to Alan's turned back, "I did not expect to finish up lying on my back in a room that smells of embrocation, soap, and hot man and wriggling out of my tights."

"Life is full of excitement," said Alan. "I'd hate for you to be bored."

"I'm going to look at that ankle now," said David. "I don't think there's anything else wrong with you that a day of bed rest won't cure."

"I don't do days in bed," she said. "An occasional lie-in in a morning does me." *Especially if there's someone with me,* she thought.

David was now holding her ankle, turning it slightly, stroking her ankle bones with his two thumbs. It hurt a bit -- but not a lot. Eventually he nodded. "I'm pretty sure this is nothing but a bad sprain," he said, "And with the experience I have with happenings like this, I ought to be right. To follow protocol, I should send you to the hospital A and E unit for an X-ray where you'd probably have to hang around for hours while the drunks get treated. But I won't. I'm going to strap this up, lend you a pair of crutches from the club store, and send you home with some pain killers." He frowned. "Do you live alone?"

"I can stay the night if you like," Alan said. "Sleep on your couch."

"I do have a spare bedroom," she said in her best freezing voice. "But thank you, that would be kind if you don't mind."

David hadn't finished doctoring. "Sprained ankles don't mend themselves quickly. You should be able to move about with the crutches, but not too far and not too fast. Don't push yourself, don't go to work for a couple of days, take as much rest as possible. Change the dressing every day."

"What about driving?" she asked.

He looked at her with that doctorly look that said she was being an idiot. "Your right foot is used for both accelerator and brake," he said. "Just for a minute, imagine you are driving your car. Move your foot as if you are accelerating and then braking."

She did. "Ow," she said, and meant it.

"Quite. No, no driving for at least a week."

Before she could ask any more questions there was a knock at the door. Alan went to open it. After a mumbled conversation, he let Sir Arthur Oswald inside. Sir Arthur looked at David. "All right to interrupt, doctor?"

"All right. Our patient is doing well."

Sir Arthur came over to look at her, shook his head, and said, "What a welcome. You'll not want to visit us again."

"In fact I will. I was telling, Alan, I was thinking of asking if I could join."

"That would be splendid. I'll propose you myself. I know you are a busy woman and this accident will affect your work. I'm going to look into the cause of your fall and..."

Jane knew where he was heading. "Sir Arthur, the fall was entirely my own fault. The club is in no way to blame and under no consideration would I consider any kind of legal action against it."

He looked down at her approvingly. "You read my mind."

"I'm a business woman."

"Indeed you are." He offered her his hand to shake. "When you have fully recovered perhaps we could have lunch together."

"I'd like that."

Sir Arthur was gone

Chapter Eight

With the crutches and Alan standing close by her, she managed to move to his car. It was slow and it was painful but it was possible. Carefully he drove her back home, making sure he didn't shake her by turning, accelerating, or braking too fast.

She had her fob in her bag, so Alan drove into the garage and parked in her spare space. They took the lift to her flat and he helped her to a couch.

"This is all a mess," she said. "I could have done without it."

"So could I. Jane, I saw you about to fall and there was nothing I could do to stop you. I felt..."

"Alan! It happened. It was no one's fault. Please don't start treating yourself to a guilt trip, I'm not in the mood right now." Then she felt ashamed of what she had said. "Why did I say that?" she asked. "I didn't mean it."

He sat beside her on the couch and put his arm around her shoulders. "You're in shock. David warned me there might be emotional upsets for no good reason. He thought when he was treating you it might have been better if you hadn't been quite so determined to be tough. It took a bit extra out of you. Now it's just your body trying to cope. That's why he wanted to be sure there was someone here with you. You might feel like crying in a moment."

"I haven't cried in years and don't propose to start now!" Even as she spoke she felt the tears trying to burst out. *Ridiculous.*

Alan did the very best thing possible: nothing. He eased her toward him and put his other arm round her waist. He didn't try to squeeze or kiss her, he just held her. Her head rested on his shoulder. He didn't even speak, which was good.

Jane sobbed for a while and then started to feel like a fool. Then she felt better. All those people claiming a good cry eases things were right.

She was not in pain, well not too much, the pain killers were very effective. She lifted her head from Alan's shoulder to sit up straight on the couch. She wiped her eyes, back to being herself again.

"I need to think," she said. "There are decisions I have to make."

"Are you hungry?"

She looked at him as if he was mad. "Hungry?"

"You promised us supper. How long since you ate?"

Good Lord, he was right. She hadn't eaten for hours. "There's stew in the pan on the hob. Afterward there's ice cream in the freezer and fresh fruit salad in the fridge. I'll just go and..."

"Sit here and do nothing. Doctor's orders. I'll fetch the food and get us a drink. It's warm enough in here, but do you have a blanket handy?"

"A blanket?"

"Whenever you're cold or injured or lost or don't know what to do, a blanket is always a comfort."

"The chest at the bottom of my bed," she told him. "There's a red one in there."

He fetched it. A red blanket with tribal markings on it, she had bought it in Canada on a trip a couple of years ago. She hadn't been able to resist it. She huddled into it -- it was so, so soft and comfortable -- and felt better at once.

Alan served the stew, complete with oven-heated rolls. "No alcohol," he told her. "Not a good idea after an injury."

"You could have a beer or a glass of wine."

"Drink on my own? A recipe for disaster."

Her stew was good (*as always*, she thought to herself) and afterward she enjoyed the fruit and ice-cream. Then Alan fetched them a mug of tea each and that too was glorious.

"I've rejoined the human race," she announced. "Now I can start worrying properly."

"What's to worry about?"

"I told you, I'm driving to France on Saturday. I have to go by car, I've got a ton of stuff for the course. I can't ask Claude to go in my place, because it's me they want to discuss expansion with and he will be running the office here."

"Problem easily solved," said Alan. "You need a chauffeur."

"A chauffeur? Where would I find one of those that doesn't cost a fortune?"

"Might I apply for the job?"

"Alan, I'm going to be away for a week. This coming Saturday to the following Sunday. You've got a job, the firm needs its computer section. Howard isn't going to be happy at you disappearing for a whole week."

"He will. For a start, I'm entitled to holiday time and extra. I've lost count of the number of extra hours and days I've put in."

"You've lost count?"

"I exaggerate. I'm an IT man, we count everything. I'll take my laptop and be in touch with the team for a couple of hours every day. Howard will be fine."

Jane moistened her lips. "You and I could go to France together?"

"Yes. Can you think of anything nicer?"

At the moment she couldn't. A yawn caught her by surprise.

Alan noticed. "It's late and your body is still in shock," he said. "It's bedtime for you. Now I've been thinking about this and perhaps we..."

"You're coming to my bed tonight. Whatever happens, I want you by my side. I'm going to have a quick wash and clean my teeth. Then I'll climb into bed. I can manage that. I'd like you in bed with me."

"Right. Tomorrow morning I'll..."

She knew she was taking charge and perhaps it was wrong, but she was the injured one and she knew what she wanted. "Tomorrow morning, you go to work. I'll stay in bed. I'll phone Claude and ask him to come round so we can sort my day out. The day after, I'm going to be fit for work."

He shook his head. "There's no stopping you when you know what you want, is there?"

"It saves time," she said. "Can you help me to my bedroom? Then come back here and wait till I shout."

"I ought to be nearby. If you fall..."

"I've done my falling for the day. I know better now. I just want to get ready for bed by myself, Alan. A bit of quietness. If I do fall I'll yell for you." Before he left the bedroom, she added, "Travelling to France with you driving -- I'm looking forward to it. Thank you for offering."

He smiled. "I'm looking forward to it just as much as you."

If she moved slowly she found she could manage most things. She made a reasonable toilette and then climbed into bed. She didn't put on pyjamas. They might get in the way.

Alan had a very speedy wash and shouted, "This time I brought my own toothbrush." But he was naked as he climbed into bed. Apparently he too had decided pyjamas wouldn't be necessary.

They lay there, side by side, both, Jane suspected, thinking the same thing.

"How's the ankle?" he asked after a while. "Much pain?"

"It aches, but it's not too bad. If I don't move it, that is."

"If you don't move it." he echoed sadly. "That'll be hard." He leaned over and kissed her carefully on the cheek. "Night, sweetheart. Sleep well."

She knew what he was thinking and feeling, because she was thinking and feeling the same thing. There was a problem. She taught techniques of problem solving, so she looked for a solution. In fact she had been looking for a solution for quite a while. This was her problem as well as his. First, she had to stop him worrying.

"I know what you want and so do I," she murmured. "Excessive movement hurts me, but there's no reason I can't lie here, all still and quiet, while you stroke or touch or ... or anything. Then we'll both be happy."

"I don't want to hurt you."

"I don't think you will. I need you, Alan."

He was quiet for a while. Then she felt his hand stretch out, cautiously feel for her breasts. He stroked them and she felt her nipples slowly come to life. "That is so nice," she whispered.

This must have encouraged him. She felt him roll onto his side, lean over her. He kissed her first on the lips and then a series of butterfly touches over the rest of her face. He was so gentle and she loved it. He was just as gentle as his head moved further down her body and he took each breast in turn into his mouth. This was even better than before. Her nipples hardened and inside her, lower down her body, she could feel stirrings that made her heart beat faster, her breathing become deeper.

It was not like her to play a completely quiescent role in anything. She stretched out a hand, felt for his body, and discovered that he was as excited as she was. She squeezed a little and was rewarded with a gasp of joy. "You're so good to me," he panted.

"Just as you are good to me," she had to answer.

A detached part of her registered the thought that this was going much better than she had feared. He was so thoughtful, so gentle, but of course he needed -- they both needed -- more.

Alan eased aside the sheet that was all that was covering them. Taking great care not to disturb her, he moved his head down her body, kissing it softly as he did so. Then he hesitated and she knew what was worrying him. Slowly, carefully, she spread her legs apart.

He sighed. "Jane, are you sure..."

"Yes, I am sure. You won't hurt me. Kiss me there?"

He did and it was good. She thought it might be just for a minute or two but soon she realised what he wanted to happen. She thought she was being selfish, she ought to stop him, but she just could not. Her breathing was coming even faster, her heart beating so hard. And then, half-unanticipated, the climax throbbed through her body, she could feel it everywhere and she moaned with joy.

She told him how good it had been, what a lover he was. Then she felt him start to move away. "Alan, there's you yet. You have to, I want you to..."

"I can't, I daren't. I might hurt you."

"You won't. Anyway, it's a risk I'm willing to take. Alan, please come back to me."

She felt him climbing over her so gently till he was leaning, poised over her. "Now," she whispered, "now." Slowly they became one.

It didn't take long. She knew by the gasp, the cry of joy that all was well for him. Then, still so gently, he stretched up to kiss her face again. Then he lay by her side. "Night, sweetheart," he said.

*****

Saturday morning and they were setting out for France. It might be a business trip, but Jane was going to enjoy it like a holiday.

Alan had stayed the night so they could set off early. In bed, once again he had made love to her in the same gentle, careful fashion that he had before. She loved it.

She was an experienced traveller. Preparation was all. Her car had been given a garage check and loaded with everything for the course. Claude had presented her with a folder with all the documents she might need and a briefing for the new work that the Tours College was asking for. She had her passport and other papers to hand. Clothes for all possible occasions were in a wheelie case and a small overnight bag for the ferry.

They drove out of town and headed for the motorway. Alan was driving with his usual care, but every now and again he took his hand off the wheel and stroked her thigh. "I'm going on holiday with a gorgeous girl," he sang. "We're sailing overnight on a boat to foreign parts."

She could tell his delight wasn't false. He really was looking forward to this, almost as an adventure. Rather sadly, she remembered that he was so much younger than her, there was so much that she had experienced and learned, but that he still had to come. It was not something that they could do together.

They took it easy on the last stages of the trip as there was little point in arriving at the terminal too early. Eventually they were in the queue, waiting to embark. She had bought an additional ticket for him, the paperwork was all in order.

"I've travelled abroad on trains, buses, and planes," she told him, "but there is no magic like waiting to board a ship."

He looked at the white side of their ferry boat stretching high above them. "I think I can see what you mean."

"You must be tired, you've driven quite a way. We'll have dinner as soon as the ship's restaurant opens and then if you like we can have an early night. First I want to stay on deck and listen to the seagulls, and watch the other ships and the coast line disappear till there's only the moon and the sea."

"Now that does sound magical. Could we sit near one of the bars and perhaps have a glass of wine each?"

She smiled happily at him. "Of course we can, as long as we are sitting outside."

Eventually it was their turn to board. They drove through the great doors of the hold, rattled to a halt, and made their way upward to collect their key.

Their cabin was an ensuite and luxurious. First Jane peered out of the porthole and then Alan helped her pull the double bed together. Soon she would be sleeping there with him, being held by him, and feeling the rumble and faint vibration of the ship's engines. Wonderful.

It was dusk now, so they left their cabin and found a bar with a few tables on the deck outside. Alan fetched them a glass of wine each and they sat and watched. Fifteen minutes later it was properly dark and they were well out to sea.

"Ready for dinner?" she asked.

"When you are. I'd like an early night. I'm feeling the effects of just one day's driving and I gather tomorrow we drive even further."

Jane looked at him demurely. "It's as good an excuse as any."

They both slept well. Early next morning Alan got up with her and accompanied her so they could watch the approach to San Malo. Jane was glad of his company, she still needed a steadying hand on stairs and narrow passages. They watched, had a Continental breakfast, and then it was time to pack the few things they'd got out and go down to the car.

As ever, Jane was thrilled because this was abroad, even the air smelled, felt different. They followed a route she had taken before. It took a while to get out of town but after that the roads were fast all the way to Tours.

"You're enjoying yourself, I can tell," said Alan as they sat outside a café and had their first holiday coffee. "There's a new sparkle to your eyes."

At least he hadn't told her she looked younger. She shrugged. "This may be a business trip but I feel as if it's a holiday. There are problems at home, with me being me and you being you, but here it's just the two of us and we can be together. We can forget the problems."

"That suits me just fine, even if I don't see as many problems back home as you do. Maybe by the end of this trip, you won't either."

It was a fair distance to Tours but the roads were quiet and the weather was good so they both enjoyed the drive. By mid afternoon, they reached the city. Jane directed Alan to the college, where she had arranged for there to be porters expecting them, ready to unload and store the workbooks. Then on they went to the city centre where they were booked in at the Hotel de St Honore. In case of gossip, she had booked a room for Alan but it was next door to hers. She suggested he leave clothes in his bedroom, and also disturb the bed.

They had both travelled in casual clothes, but they were meeting Giselle for dinner, so Jane wanted to be slightly formal. After showering she put on a dark brown silk dress, that she thought suited her very well. Perhaps it was a little low cut -- but they were in France. Normally, for business, she wore minimal jewellery. She believed it could detract from what she was saying. But this evening she put on an amber necklace. It was an attractive, eye-catching piece. She wanted to look well.

She was impressed when Alan came into her room. He was wearing a light grey suit with a white silk shirt and a conservative tie. She had never seen him dressed this way before. He looked what he was, a smart, shrewd, professional man.

"You look very good," she told him. "I'm proud to be seen with you."

He grinned. "Not half as proud as I am to be seen with you. When we get downstairs, I'll be watching the men staring at you and feeling envious of me."

"Sometimes I think you have a silver tongue!"

*****

Jane thought she must have been slightly dim. Giselle was a hard worker, she spoke excellent English, was bright, and attractive. She was also aged about thirty and recently divorced. She had expected Alan to like Giselle. She didn't realise that Giselle might like Alan quite a lot.

Giselle was already in the bar. She too had made an effort as no one dined in the Hotel de St Honore unless they were well dressed. This was a place to be seen. She wore a crimson silk top and a rather short black skirt. Jane reflected with some envy that she couldn't wear a skirt so short. Not at her age. For a moment she felt dissatisfied.

Giselle and Jane kissed each other, Jane explained her fall and how she could not drive. Giselle was desolated for her. Jane introduced Alan as a lecturer in computing who had agreed to act as her chauffeur. In Giselle's eyes she saw an instant flash of interest. Yes, she really should have expected that.

A waiter came over and as Jane studied the proffered list of wines, Giselle chatted to Alan. She half listened to the conversation. Giselle had read an article by Alan in one of the computing magazines and was vastly impressed by it. Alan, like all authors, was only too pleased to talk about it.

They started with a bottle of local Loire wine. The food was excellent, too good to be interfered with by talk about work. They'd save that for later. The chat was general -- but with a definite leaning toward computers and their workings. Jane would have been pleased that Alan was enjoying himself if she hadn't also realised that Giselle was rather obviously hanging on his every word.

When they returned to the bar, Jane ordered another bottle and got down to business with Giselle. She had been in touch with the college, they were specific about what they wanted. Giselle could offer it and they liked her. So far so good. The extra hours and payment took a little more negotiating, but was agreed amicably. Jane said she'd send Giselle a contract by the end of the week.

Normally, Jane would then have spent a little time chatting on non-work subjects, but this evening she apologised and said that they had been travelling for two days and she was very tired, so she hoped Giselle would excuse her. Alan chipped in and said the same.

Giselle was instantly solicitous. Before parting, Jane told her she'd be at the college talking to the director for the next three days and would like to drop in to watch her work. This was her normal practice as all her contract staff knew. Giselle said she wouldn't be working tomorrow, but any other time would be fine. They wished each other an enthusiastic goodnight and parted.

Alan went to his room to change. Half an hour later her door opened and he slipped in, in his dressing gown. Jane was reading in bed. He locked the door and climbed in with her.

"It has been a long two days," he said, "just how tired are you?"

"Not that tired," she replied, and reached out for him.

The next morning, Alan rose early to go back to his own room to unmake the bed and leave signs of having slept there. Later, fully dressed, he tapped on her door and they went down for a swift breakfast. As they drank coffee and buttered croissants, he said, "There was a message left on my room phone last night from Giselle. She said she had been thinking. She knew that all I had to do tomorrow is drive you to the college, leave you there, do a bit of sightseeing and then return for you in the late afternoon. I'd told her I didn't have anything planned apart from logging into work and checking all was well."

"Yes?" said Jane.

Alan pulled a chunk off his croissant. "She said I might be lost in a new city, so would I like to meet her for lunch and she could show me round a little."

Jane felt a stirring of alarm. "Are you going to meet her?" she asked, trying to indicate that it was all one to her.

"That's up to you. What do you think?"

"Alan, it's not up to me. You have a perfect right to meet up if you'd like to. If she was a male lecturer and offered you a tour of the city, would you have accepted?"

He thought for a minute. Then he said, "Yes. All right, I will."

Jane tried very hard not to show this was the wrong answer.

Chapter Nine

The next day Alan drove her to the college, asked her if she was sure she had all the paperwork she needed. Asking her that! He still didn't know her very well. She told him to have a good time with Giselle (*but not too good*, she thought to herself) and repeated that she would phone him when she was finished for the day. "I suppose you don't want me to kiss you goodbye?" he asked.

"Not outside the college. Well, yes I do, but I'm not going to let you. This is business, Alan."

"Business," he sighed. Before driving away he walked her to the college office and made sure that she was welcomed.

She was early. After profuse apologies she was invited to sit in a side room to wait where coffee would be provided. She quite liked this chance to get her thoughts in order. She had loved every minute of being with Alan for the past two days, but when she was with him she couldn't think about him, or him and her together, in a detached way. In the light of recent uncomfortable feelings, she rather thought she needed to.

He was going to meet Giselle and Jane wasn't happy about it. She wished he hadn't agreed but it would be against all her principles to say so. After all, she'd been the one to propose that they kept things casual for a year. The thing was, she hadn't expected to feel jealous. Take it a step further. How would she feel if he fell for Giselle? It could very easily happen. They were of similar age and interests, and both were attractive. Even considering the possibility made her stomach clench. Not to put too fine a point on it, she'd be horrendously upset. This was perfectly ridiculous. She'd only known him for two weeks. Women of her age and maturity didn't fall for very much younger men. They were called cougars -- figures of fun who were laughed at. She didn't want to be laughed at, but she didn't want to give up Alan either.

She was glad when the director's secretary came to collect her. Now she could think of something different.

*****

Jane spent most of the day in detailed negotiation with the college director and the Head of Business Studies. Unlike other French firms she had dealt with, they did not stop for a lengthy lunch. Sandwiches and a salad were served as they talked. By the end of the day, all three of them were pleased with how far they got.

She phoned Alan and he picked her up promptly. It was quite

funny, both of them were eager to hear about the other's day. Politely, he let her talk first.

"I had a good day. It went well. We were agreed on general principles. All we have to do now is go through the little points that can aggravate later if they're not sorted out first."

He nodded approvingly. "Just like computer software. I like it."

"With any luck we might even finish the business tomorrow. How was your lunch with Giselle?"

"I quite enjoyed it."

"What did you talk about?" she asked as casually as she could.

"Computer stuff mostly. She's a bright girl, Jane, has some good ideas."

"Nothing else important?"

He reached over and squeezed her thigh. "I know why you're asking. She told me about her messy divorce and how she was off men for good."

Jane made an ambiguous noise. "And you believed her?"

"Not a word of it. She kissed me as we said goodbye but it wasn't half as much fun as being kissed by you. She also asked if I was doing anything this evening. Did I expect to have to spend it with you, for example. If not perhaps we could meet for a drink together?"

Jane was beginning to have some very grim thoughts about Giselle.

Alan laughed. "Take that look off your face. I said it sounded very nice, but I had brought my laptop with me and having had a day off today, I now had to get in touch with my firm and see how they were doing without me. She understood at once."

"Good. She had no suspicions about us, then? She doesn't think we are in any way a pair?"

"No suspicions at all. In fact, she said..." His voice trailed away.

"I get worried when people leave sentences half finished. She said what, Alan?" Jane heard herself using her sharp lecturer's voice, but couldn't help it.

He waited a minute before he answered. "She asked what it was like having to spend so much time with a woman who, though very pleasant, was so much older than me."

"And you answered?"

"That age has nothing to do with how interesting a person is, nor how easy they are to get on with. I told her we had a professional relationship and that you were much more pleasant to work for than some other people I know."

"A good answer," said Jane. "Sorry."

"It even has the merit of being true. Can we drop this now, please? Did I hear you say that you might finish off the negotiations with the college by tomorrow night?"

"You did."

"And we don't set off back until Saturday. That means we have three days to ourselves. A holiday."

"I hadn't thought of it like that," she said. "We ought to keep Wednesday free in case something comes up, and there is work waiting for me back at home, but ... yes, we could have a little holiday."

"Looking forward to it already," he said.

So was she.

*****

They had dinner again downstairs and then retired to her room. Jane typed up all the notes on today's meetings on her laptop while Alan put in a couple of hours work on his own, phoning his second in command when there was something he didn't agree with. He'd promised Howard that he would keep in touch with the work and she was impressed at how easy it was for him. If he had fifteen minutes to himself and all the facts he could apparently solve problems with no trouble. "How do you manage to work so quickly?" she asked him.

"I don't get in touch with people unless I desperately have to. Mostly I talk to the computer."

Well yes, she was doing that too, but mostly she had a horrible suspicion it was because his mind was that much more agile, that much younger. Jane was efficient, but Alan flew.

Every now and then one of them would stand, wander round the room and, in passing, kiss or touch the other. Just a friendly kiss, a tiny stroke. It was a revelation how much she loved just being with him.

Next morning, Alan ran her to the college and said he was going to look around the town on his own today, though naturally he'd rather do it with her. When she was ready she was to phone him as she had yesterday and he'd pick her up fifteen minutes later.

The planning meeting went well, they were all anxious to reach agreement so there was a fair amount of give and take. The director apologised that today there were some visiting academic staff and he would have to eat lunch with them. Jane said she would happily go to the students' dining room. She also mentioned that she'd like to see Giselle working. This was speedily arranged.

For a moment or two she watched through the glass door, observing Giselle's class. Much could be learned by the body language in a class and the faces of the students. Giselle was taking a beginners' computing course, which meant she had to move from student to student. Jane could tell she was good at her job.

After a while she knocked on the door and was invited in. Giselle suggested she walk round and observe, the students wouldn't mind. She did this and she was satisfied. She could tell the students were satisfied too.

It was a natural progression to join Giselle for lunch.

"I enjoyed showing Alan around yesterday," Giselle started off by saying. "He's a new lecturer as well as your driver, isn't he?"

"He can only work for me part-time, and he doesn't usually drive me at all, but yes, I believe he'll be an asset to the company."

"I'm sure he will be. He is so knowledgeable about so many things. I showed him all my favourite places and I do not think we stopped talking at all. It was a great day." Giselle played with her salade Nicoise. "Do you know anything about him personally, Jane?"

Jane looked at her sharply. "His referees all think highly of him. Why are you interested?"

Giselle seemed entirely unembarrassed. "He told me he's not married. Do you know if he is seeing anyone? Living with anyone?"

Somehow Jane kept her face impassive. She hadn't expected a direct question. She took a mouthful of iced Vittel water before she answered. She couldn't tell Giselle the truth and she didn't want to lie. She liked the girl and really wanted to keep her on her staff. "I'm sorry, I can't discuss the private life of my staff unless they want me to," she said. "It wouldn't be fair. You wouldn't like it if someone was asking about you, would you?"

Giselle gave a Gallic shrug. "It depends who was asking," she said with devastating frankness. Then she caught Jane's expression and said, "No, I suppose not."

"All I can say is that he's never mentioned any young woman that he is interested in," said Jane stiffly. This was not a lie. Jane was not a young woman.

Giselle smiled widely. "Then there's a chance for me. I've given him my e-mail address and my phone number. He can get in touch if he likes. Is there any chance of him coming to Tours to lecture?"

"None. His French is school-level."

"That is a shame. He is beautiful, yes? He was polite of course, but he kept looking at me in that way ... you must have had it happen to you when you were younger. A man looking at you as if you were all the world to him?"

"Oh, yes, that way," said Jane. She felt hurt and upset, firstly by what Giselle was saying -- because after all, why wouldn't Alan find Giselle attractive, young and beautiful and clever as she was -- and secondly, stupidly, by the fact that Giselle was treating her as old.

The young woman peeped prettily up at her. "So you would have no objection if I was to see more of him? And if he does ask about me, you can tell him I am a good worker, yes?"

This was getting worse. "Giselle, the last thing I need to worry about is the love life of my staff. I'll tell him I think you are a lovely person, if the subject comes up. Will that do?"

"Thank you so much," Giselle beamed at her.

Jane looked at the rest of her lunch and pushed it away uneaten.

*****

It was a good thing they had already come to a complete accord as to how Jane and the college were to work together, because she didn't think she'd have been able to concentrate otherwise. This afternoon, it was simply a question of signing the contracts. Hands were shaken all round. Jane felt as if her face was going to crack with the effort of keeping the fake smile in place. How could she bear this? It was everything she didn't want.

As arranged Alan picked her up. It was a fine day, the sky was blue and there was that feeling of warm late summer in the air.

"I've been talking to people and inside buildings all day," she told him. "Can we just drive out into the country where it's quiet and peaceful and people aren't making trouble for me without trying?"

"Has it been that bad? No problem, I'll get out of the city, find a quiet spot and we can sit in the sun and when you're ready you can tell me about it." He reached for her hand, lifted it to his lips, and kissed it.

He must have been studying the map. In no time at all they were in the countryside, bouncing down a narrow track that ended on the river edge. There was a great circle of trees with benches under them. He parked and they strolled over to one. There were no people around.

The benches had high backs and sides. Alan told her to sit with her back propped against the side and her feet stretched out in front of her, her hands in her lap. "Now close your eyes," he said. "Take a deep breath through your nose ... hold it ... and slowly let it out of your mouth. Now again ... breathe in ... hold it ... slowly, slowly, breathe out. Now as you breathe out, feel all the tension in your muscles, in your body, disappearing too."

He repeated this several times and she followed his instructions. To her astonishment, she began to feel relaxed, feel that the world wasn't too full of problems.

"Why don't you doze for a while?" he asked. "Lift your feet up, put them here on my lap, and I'll take your shoes off, stroke your feet."

"All right," she said. She wouldn't have let him take her shoes off when she first sat on the bench, but now she did, and the stroking was blissfully calming. She didn't go to sleep, rather lapsing into a half trance.

They both remained silent for a quarter of an hour but then she stirred, feeling much more herself.

"You didn't tell me you were a hypnotist," she said.

"I'm not. That technique was taught me by a pal who had a really bad heart condition. The minute he felt his body or his brain being overloaded, that was what he did. It worked for him, he thought it had saved his life. Now, we can wait if you prefer, but if you want to tell me what's troubling you, I'd like to try and help."

She sighed. "That's a bit of a joke, because you're the cause of the trouble. Well, part of the cause. The part that caused it is the part that I like best about you."

"What? Can you make sense of that sentence? I can't."

She had to laugh, though she didn't really feel like it. "Alan, you're a very attractive man in all sorts of ways. That's the part I like. Unfortunately, so does Giselle. She has fallen for you, wants to see more of you, asked me if I'd mind if the two of you got together. She asked if I knew whether you had any other ladies in mind. I didn't lie. I said you hadn't told me of any." Then, deliberately, she added, "She didn't mind asking me as I am so much older. Can you imagine how that made me feel?"

Jane had to give Alan credit for his reaction, there was no pride in male conquest in his voice. "I'm aware Giselle is attracted to me, of course, but I didn't intend it to happen. She's clever. We have a lot of things in common. She is amusing company. I like her. However, in no way did I give her any cause to think that ... that we had a future."

"Perhaps not on purpose." Jane remembered the words Giselle had used to describe what she herself might once have experienced "before she became older." "I've got to ask, Alan. Did you look at her as if, and I quote, she was 'all the world to you'?"

The silence between them grew. Then, "I might have, by accident," he said with a sigh. "I was talking to her, but thinking about you. I guess, looking back, it might have been misleading. I didn't mean to, Jane. I wanted to be friendly."

"I've seen you look at me the way she described."

"In your case I mean it," he shouted then moderated his tone. "Sorry. I'm sorry. Oh, Jane, this is a terrible mistake and I'm sorry if Giselle has been hurt but it's you I love. You know that, don't you?"

Yes, she did, and she was rather afraid she loved him too. But he was an attractive, intelligent man with a zest for living life to the full, as well as working. How would she bear it when she saw the love in his eyes fade and turn to someone else?

They stayed another few minutes on the river bank and then drove to the nearest village and sat in the sun outside a café, drinking coffee.

She needed to think about the immediate future. Strictly speaking, her work in Tours was now over. There was nothing to prevent them setting off back for England the next day. Given her gut reaction to Alan's possible involvement with another woman, this was exactly what they should do. They should go straight home and break off the relationship, so she would never again have to experience this desperate work-sapping desolation.

She opened her mouth to say as much, knowing it would ruin his holiday. He turned his head and smiled directly into her eyes -- and to her total astonishment she heard herself say, "I don't want to go home. I know I should, I know I have work to do, but I want to stay in France with you."

"Funny you should say that. I was thinking exactly the same thing. We can, you know, we both have laptops and no one is expecting us until the weekend."

Jane Gray, you are an utter fool. You are building up pain for yourself.

"Do you want to stay in Tours?" she asked.

"No. I like the place no end, but if we stay here, Giselle will try to get in touch with me. And for everyone's sake I think it best if we don't see each other."

"True," agreed Jane. "So where would you like to go for our tiny stolen holiday?"

"Let's drive back to the coast tomorrow. It means we don't have to spend two days just driving. I would love to look round St Malo and I've always fancied a trip to Mont St Michel. It's quite close."

"I've never seen it either. That's a great idea."

A look of solicitous care settled on Alan's face. "It'll be a long trip tomorrow. You've been working like fury for the past two days. We've already established you're tired. How about going back to the hotel, having a quick dinner, and going to bed quite early?"

Jane stretched and smiled. "You've talked me into it."

*****

Driving to St Malo next day, Jane felt odd, though she couldn't put her finger on why. On the face of it, she should be very happy: her ankle was feeling better, Alan's hand rested on her thigh at regular intervals and when they were occasionally stopped by traffic he leaned over and kissed her on the cheek. Professionally speaking, the trip to Tours had been a complete success. There was nothing like a full order book to put a smile on a woman's face. So why did she still have a sense of unease?

They talked as they travelled, about the differences in the towns and villages, about how there always seemed to be more countryside in France than in England. "This is lovely," said Alan. "I'm so happy to be here, with you, right now."

Then he said something that altered her mood, though she was careful not to let him know.

"Actually, Jane, you've done me a favour. Coming away on this trip has made me realise what a rut I've got into. It's not that I'm not enjoying working for Howard any more, but I'm easily on top of it and I want more out of life. I want a big meaty challenge like setting up a new system or restructuring a multi-program suite for a big multi-national."

"That would mean moving, wouldn't it?"

"Yes, but that's the advantage of a minimalist lifestyle. Relocation is easy. I love the thought of getting to grips with a new city, a new culture."

He had so much energy. It pulsed off him in waves. Jane felt weak just listening to him.

"New York," he was saying now. "Ever been to the States, Jane? I had an exchange there in my first job and it was great. My old boss has moved right up in the echelons and he sent me a feeler a month or so ago asking if I might like to go back. How d'you fancy living in New York? Could you run your business from an apartment overlooking Central Park?"

For a moment she didn't know what to say. Was he serious? And if so, did he expect her to go with him? Was he asking her to live with him? She mumbled something about perhaps she'd like a bite of the Big Apple, but only for a week or two. She was worried though. Alan was becoming alarmingly serious.

They booked into their hotel, walked along the ramparts, and then returned for dinner and another early night. Jane was beginning to get a real taste for these early nights. She'd miss them when she got home.

Next day the weather was gorgeous. Jane gazed out of the window at it while she dealt with a few early morning emails. She couldn't relax and be a proper holiday-maker until she'd checked on work.

They drove over to Mont St Michel which was as impressive as it looked. They had to park on the causeway outside, pulling in beside a British car. A giggling young couple got out, took rucksacks out of the boot, and promptly had a long languorous kiss.

Alan nudged Jane. "Isn't that wonderful? I'm sure they'll have a long happy life together."

"Just because of one kiss?"

"You didn't notice what was littered inside the boot."

"No, what was it?"

"Confetti. They are newly-weds. Isn't that nice?"

Jane shrugged. "Some people seem to find it agreeable." She set off at a brisk pace, not liking the dreamy speculative look on Alan's face. Marriage was *never* going to be for her.

The brisk pace didn't last. They weren't even a third of the way up before Jane had slowed down. Partly this was due to her ankle, but mostly she couldn't cope with the sheer physical exertion.

"Do you not do any sport?" asked Alan with a tiny frown. "No keep fit activities? Not even aerobics?"

Jane stopped for a breather on the pretext of flexing her ankle. "No, I never have time. I'm on the go with work every waking moment."

"Yes, I'd noticed," murmured Alan ruefully. "I'd go mad without a game of rugby now and again, or a good hard workout on the squash court."

"It does keep you in excellent shape," said Jane admiringly.

Alan grinned.

Even so, when they reached the top of Mont St Michel and sat outside the café drinking a citron pressé each, Jane thought it was a tiny bit unfair that she had turned brick-red from the unaccustomed exercise, yet Alan had hardly even broken into a sweat. *Younger*, whispered a nasty voice in her head. *Fitter. More energy.* And again. *Younger.*

"I like the sun," said Alan. "English winters are neither one thing nor the other. Cold weather but very little snow. I've been saving up my holiday days. Shall we have a Christmas break in the Caribbean? Plenty of swimming and sun."

"Christmas is months away!"

"So? What do you usually do for it?"

"Nothing. I use the time to catch up."

"At Christmas? That's appalling. Jane, you have to take some time off."

"Why? I feel odd when I don't work." As she was proving right now.

"You seem to be managing today."

"Yes, and you have no idea how weird it feels. Not to be doing anything for a project. Not to have paperwork to read through and sign. Not to have something going on in one corner of my head."

"Why? Why, Jane? Why are you so driven? I don't understand."

Whether it was his frustration, or the nagging feeling of things left undone, the way her legs ached from the climb or even, stupidly, the young couple's uninhibited clinch down in the car park, Jane didn't know. Perhaps it was a combination of everything building up in her. Anyway, she let fly.

"You want to know? Okay, I'll tell you. When I was first at university, all young and innocent and dewy-eyed, I fell in love. Nothing strange in that. All students do it. Except in my case, Lawrence was older, experienced, good-looking, flatteringly attentive. I fell for him like a ton of bricks. We pooled our grants to get a flat, and soon I was doing everything for him -- his cooking, his cleaning, and as it turned out, his work too. The day his wife turned up on the doorstep was not a good one."

Alan winced. "Ouch."

"Ouch, doesn't even begin to cover it. Being young and stupid, I swept out in heartbroken indignation -- and found myself homeless, penniless, and a gnat's breath away from being accused of plagiarism over the work *he* had submitted that he'd appropriated from me. I swore then that never again would I depend on a man for where I lived, what I ate, or whether I felt happy or miserable. I swore I would be rich and successful in my own right. Every single thing I've done since the day I walked out has been geared to that end."

"I can understand why, but, Jane, you've made it now. You are successful in your own right. You can take a holiday if you want one."

Jane shut her eyes for a moment, shaken by her outburst. Yes, she could take holidays now, but Alan had missed the point. Working hard was what defined her, it was what made her a person. Alan was still young, of course. He'd never known what it was to be homeless, broke, and terrified. She dragged a deep breath into her lungs.

They were interrupted by the ringing of his phone. "Giselle! Hi!" said Alan, answering. "Did we forget something?" Then, "No, I'm afraid not, we're on our way back ... No, I won't be, I only came over this time as a favour to Jane." And then, finally, "Look, I like you and I really enjoyed meeting you and I'm sorry if you got the wrong impression, but I'm not looking for any sort of relationship."

He listened, grimaced, and put the phone ruefully back in his pocket. "That went well."

"I did warn you."

"It wouldn't have happened at all if we were open about us. I'm fed up with this hole in the corner arrangement, Jane. I know how I feel about you. That's not going to change. When we get back home I want people to know we are a couple."

"We agreed we'd wait for a year. What we have at the moment is a lovely casual fling with no strings attached."

"And see where it gets us: to nice girls like Giselle being made to feel embarrassed and unhappy. A year is too long." He took her hand. "Does this honestly feel like a fling to you?"

Jane couldn't lie. "No."

"Me neither." He leaned across the table and kissed her. "Ready to carry on exploring the island?"

*****

That night, Jane lay awake for a long time after Alan gone to sleep. His arm rested across her in untroubled assurance. All Jane could see was his youth, Giselle's youth, Annette's youth. If they came out as a couple, people would note the age difference and laugh at her, just the way they'd secretly laughed at her when she was running around working her fingers to the bone for Lawrence because she was too dumb to see he was using her.

It wasn't going to happen. She wouldn't let it. She didn't want Alan ridiculed any more than she could bear to be laughed at herself. As soon as they got back to England, she'd tell him it was over.

But oh, it was going to be so hard.

Chapter Ten

It was a relief to be back at work, faced with the usual set of problems. Jane was sure dealing with work issues would keep her too busy to worry about personal decisions. She was wrong.

For a start, he assumed they would now be spending a lot more time together. He suggested they keep spare sets of clothes in each other's flats. He said things like "Where shall we eat tonight?" instead of asking whether she was free to have a meal.

Jane panicked. This week she was going to have to tell Alan about her merger. She couldn't leave it any longer. She was going to have to tell him she was going to San Francisco. She was going to have to tell him that she'd be going alone.

As ever, she consulted Claude. "Worrying about Alan is making me careless," she told him. "I'm making mistakes -- only small ones -- but I don't like it. Am I noticeably less efficient?"

His answer was honest. "To me you are. You've lost that fine edge. I doubt other people will notice."

"Not yet, maybe. They will if it carries on."

"Lighten up, Jane. A little fallibility isn't a bad thing."

"It is to me. Claude, what am I going to do about Alan? I can't bear to lose him and yet I know, ultimately, I'm not good for him."

"Give him a nice meal, tell him about the merger. You owe it to him, Jane."

"I'll tell him tonight."

With her decision made, even if it wouldn't be easy, Jane was finally able to lose herself in work. It was late afternoon when she reached out her hand to the phone to ask Claude something and realised mid-stretch that she hadn't moved from her desk for a couple of hours. She stood up, wincing at the stiffness in her muscles, and walked along the corridor to his office instead.

The door was slightly open. Inside, Jane could just hear him on the telephone. "Two o'clock tomorrow, then, Mr Worral. I'll want to look at a selection of rings in that range."

Jane smiled. Claude had been talking about buying an eternity ring for Gavin, because, he joked when his partner was being particularly difficult, it felt as if they'd been together for an eternity already.

Footsteps sounded as someone hurried around the corner. Jane's heart thumped as she saw it was Claude. So who was in his office talking about rings? Her brain had already supplied the answer before Claude spoke.

"Hi, Jane, the course Alan's designed is looking good. Do you want us to run through it for you?"

She couldn't speak. She had forgotten Alan was coming in to fine-tune his course contents with Claude. Oh dear Lord, rings. Why would Alan want to look at rings? Worral's was a jewellery shop on the high street. She'd bought a couple of pieces from there herself. It was classy and expensive.

Claude was looking at her enquiringly. She pulled herself together and shook her head. "I won't disturb you. I was going to ask you about the Mayfield contract, but it can wait."

She went back to her office, very perturbed indeed.

*****

The rest of the afternoon passed by rote. Jane didn't trust herself with anything bar routine matters. To all intents and purposes she was deep in a spreadsheet when Alan knocked on her door an hour later.

"Jane, I'm sorry, I've been called back. Something's cropped up, and it looks as if it'll be an all-nighter. I'll make up for it tomorrow, I promise."

"No need to apologise," she said briskly. "Both of us are busy, committed people. At least if you're trouble-shooting you won't be bored."

"True, but I wouldn't have been bored spending the evening with you either. I was going to ask you something."

Jane spread her palms. "Ask away."

His cheeks flushed slightly. "I'll leave it until tomorrow evening."

"Okay. Off you go and save the universe."

He grinned. "Not quite that, though you wouldn't think so, the way Howard's going on." He looked at her uncertainly, but she didn't lift her cheek to be kissed, so after a tiny hesitation he left.

Jane listened to his footsteps retreating down the corridor then lowered her head onto her arms. Playing it cool then had been the most difficult thing she'd done for weeks. She was Jane Gray, owner and managing director of a thriving business, known and respected by colleagues and clients alike. She was tough, decisive, and logical. All she wanted to do right now was go home and pull the bedclothes over her head. What was she to do about Alan?

Except, of course, she knew what to do, and that was the cause of her unhappiness.

*****

The next morning she was discussing the handover details with her business agent in London. As she talked, she looked with satisfaction around her office, at the tasteful, subtly powerful furnishings (care of Claude's Gavin), at the certificates on the wall, at the slightly open office door letting in the distant background sound of her people at work.

She suddenly sat bolt upright. Her office door was open. Anyone could have overheard her, the same as she had overheard Alan. That would be horribly premature -- she hadn't let the staff know about the merger yet, and before that it was imperative that she tell Alan.

She made up her mind. She crossed swiftly to Claude's office. Fortunately there was no one with him. "Can you hold the fort this afternoon? I need to go to Worral's Jewellers."

"Of course," said Claude. "Buying something nice?"

"Far from it," she said unhappily. "I'm going to stop Alan from buying anything. I overheard him yesterday asking to look at rings."

Claude made an impatient noise. "Sometimes I want to knock your heads together. Have you even *tried* talking this all through with him?"

"There's a park opposite the shop. We can sit there and talk."

"About time too. Try to take as well as give, Jane. Let me know what happens."

"I will. I think I may need tea and sympathy afterwards."

It was a fine, late-summer's day. Jane thought this was singularly unfair. She would have preferred it to be dark, cold, and raining to match her mood. This was going to be one of the worst meetings of her life.

It was a quarter to two, she was standing outside Worral's Jewellers. She had looked inside, Alan wasn't there. She peered at a display of necklaces that didn't in the least interest her. At regular intervals she glanced up and down the street. Suppose he'd cancelled? Or rearranged the time?

Then she saw him striding down the street. It hurt her that she was going to take that bounce out of his step. She turned and stepped into the middle of the pavement. He stopped, his eyes widened with delight. "Jane! What are you doing here?"

"I could ask you the same question, but I have a nasty feeling I don't need to." She took him by the arm. "We can sit in the park over there. We need to talk, Alan."

"But I was going to..." Then he realised. "This meeting isn't an accident is it?"

"No, it's not. I overheard you on the phone yesterday." For the past few hours she had wondered how this meeting would go, what would be the best approach, the kindest way to explain things. She had come to no firm conclusion. She was just going to wing it. "Alan, before you do anything that you and I might both regret, you've got to listen to me."

He was silent as she guided him across the road and over to a bench. Then he spoke. "So, you overheard me asking Worral's about rings and leapt to the conclusion I was going there to buy an engagement ring and ask you to marry me. Is that right?"

"I hadn't gone that far, but I do know a ring is a very personal piece of jewellery, and if it *was* for me then there are things you need to know before you buy it."

"I don't understand why you are so against the idea, Jane. I love you and I know you love me. I'm not taking you for granted, like that idiot Lawrence. I'm not belittling you or stealing from you or laughing at you. I want to share my life with you. I want us to go forward together. I was going to invite you to my mother's birthday party and propose to you there, surrounded by all the people I grew up with, to show you I was serious."

Jane's mouth fell open in horror. "Alan! You were going to ruin your mother's birthday party by standing up in front of all her friends and asking a woman thirteen years older than you to marry you?"

"Ah, I hadn't thought of it that way round. Bad idea, yes?"

"Very bad idea. If she didn't hate me already, she certainly would after that."

"So will you? Marry me?"

Jane looked down at her lap, where her hands had twisted together so tightly she wasn't sure she could unclench them. "No." She swallowed painfully. "I'm too old for you, Alan. Just that last wonderful, disastrous idea of yours proves it. I don't want to be your keeper. I don't want to save you from not thinking things through. I love you too much for that."

He gave a short, mirthless laugh. "Thank you. I think. At least you've stopped pretending what we have is just a fling."

"It was never a fling," she admitted. "I said that so when you got bored, it would give us both an easy way out without losing face. The trouble is, you're moving too fast to get bored. So I'm calling a halt, Alan. I won't let you ruin your life."

"You think you not marrying me is going to stop me ruining my life? I could go back to playing rugby and get injured. I could climb a mountain and fall down an inaccessible gully. I could drive at a hundred and fifty miles an hour down the motorway. All those would do it."

"Yes, but none of them would be directly my fault."

Alan stood up, took a restless pace forward and another one back. "Your computer course, Jane. I'll give this one for you, but no more. I can't be with you and not be *with* you."

"There's no need to worry about that," said Jane wearily. "This is the other thing I should have told you before, but I didn't want to spoil what we had. Alan, my firm is merging with Walter G Traekel. He's paying me an absurd amount of money for the name and for the operation. I'm going to be a director of the parent company and I'm going to San Francisco to work in their global arm for a year. Claude is taking over at the helm here, although I still will be in overall charge and I'll be working closely with him."

He was completely silent. The three feet that separated them seemed like three miles.

"This is it?" he said at last. "Right now? Not even one last beautiful night to remember each other by?"

It would have been so easy to agree to having one last beautiful night. Love and sorrow and pity nearly overcame Jane. It took all the strength she possessed to stay strong. "If I did that, I'd never let go. Walter says I can travel over whenever I like. I think for both our sakes I'm going to ask for it to be soon."

"I love you, Jane."

"I love you too, Alan. That's why I'm going to stand up and leave. I'm sorry. Look after yourself."

She was glad that he couldn't see the tears in her eyes as she walked away.

*****

"How did it go?" asked Claude, handing her a large mug of hot tea as soon as she stepped over the threshold.

"It could only go badly. I think he understands. I don't know."

"So what are you going to do now?"

"I'm going to e-mail Walter and tell him I'm coming to start work in San Francisco in a fortnight. We can arrange you taking over from me in that time, can't we?"

"Most of it is already done. I'll miss you, Jane."

"I'll miss you too, but we'll be in touch the whole time."

"And Alan? Will you miss him?"

She shut her eyes briefly. "More than life itself."

Epilogue

She stared out of the window as her terminal recognised the password and produced the array of instructions, questions, and messages that would occupy her for the first hours of the day. Her work. Sometimes she wondered if the computer was really the greatest invention of the past hundred and fifty years.

Then she blinked. Her terminal was playing a tune: "I've got you under my skin!" Where was that coming from? She looked at the screen and there was a cartoon figure, a vast muscled man in a bathing costume. He was dancing and singing and his muscles danced in time to the music. Memories came flooding back. After she had spent that first night with Alan he had sent her this cartoon message and it had both angered and amused her. As before, the figure now pointed downward. There was a message waiting for her. From Alan.

Without thinking, she reached for the terminal and hit the pause switch. The figure stopped dancing. She fancied it looked at her despondently,

Alan was sending her a message. Was she strong enough to read it yet? Did she want to read it?

They hadn't corresponded for four months. He was still doing some lecturing for the company. Claude had persuaded him, he'd said. He insisted on telling her how Alan was, even though she'd told him she wanted a clean break. She might just as well have saved her breath.

Now Alan was trying to get in touch. She could easily wipe out the message without reading it. For ten minutes she ignored it, and felt that the figure stared at her accusingly.

She had a good life here. She was enjoying it. The only problems she had were work related and she could cope with them. Did she want to return to the anxiety she had felt so often when she was with Alan? Ahem, said her conscience, what about the great joy he had brought her? She had tried to put that out of her mind. But from time to time, sometimes at night when she couldn't sleep, sometimes when work got a little too complex -- she remembered drinking wine with him, chatting to him, being in bed with him, and it hurt.

She didn't like unfinished business. She turned to the terminal and looked at the message that the dancing figure was pointing to.

> *I've just dropped Mother at the airport for a holiday with her bridge-playing girlfriends. As I stood in the terminal building, I remembered coming down to meet you in London at two minutes' notice. Four*

months apart and I'm still missing you, Jane. I think you're using the age gap as an excuse because you're afraid of being hurt again. Well, I'm hurting now. I can't see that it is ever going to stop.

You've made it, Jane, don't you see? You're rich. You're successful. Now you need to make your inner self as successful as your outer self. Release yourself from that emotional straightjacket. My plane lands at San Francisco airport at twenty-two minutes past three this afternoon. I'm booked into the Bay View Hotel for the next week. Nobody knows us in the States, Jane. Walk tall, dress magnificently, and let's celebrate being a couple. Pain just shows you you're alive. I don't see any other reason for letting it go on.

Love you so much, Alan.

Jane was laughing and crying all at once. Oh how she'd missed his energy, his conviction that there was a happy ending in all things. For once, she wasn't going to reason her way out of this. Sometimes the wild shots hit home. She told her secretary she would be away from her desk all afternoon and would she order a taxi to get her to the airport by three thirty. Decision made.

The End

About Roger Sanderson

I was a College Lecturer in Liverpool for thirty years, teaching English Literature during the week and rock-climbing at the weekend. I still live in Liverpool and also have a static caravan a two hour drive away in the Lake District where I go to work as often as I can. In it I write easily. It inspires me when I sit on my decking with the mountains behind me and Ullswater in the distance below. If I can't write, then I walk.

My writing career started when I wrote scripts for Commando comics - stories of the Second World War. I followed that by writing forty-four Medical Romances for Harlequin Mills and Boon, which I really enjoyed and which are being reissued by Accent Press. Now I'm concentrating on longer romantic comedy books. Love and laughter - what could be better?

When I'm not writing, I like to travel. Mostly I tour Europe, but every couple of years I get in a visit to the West Coast of America for walking of a totally different kind.

Made in the USA
Charleston, SC
20 December 2015